LOVE'S SACRIFICE

Mystic Hope Series
Book One: Unbroken Spirit
Book Two: Love's Sacrifice

LOVE'S SACRIFICE
BOOK TWO IN THE MYSTIC HOPE SERIES

By Kelsey Norman

Love's Sacrifice
Published by Mountain Brook Ink
White Salmon, WA U.S.A.

The website addresses shown in this book are not intended in any way to be or imply an endorsement on the part of Mountain Brook Ink, nor do we vouch for their content.

Scripture quotations are taken from the King James Version of the Bible. Public domain.
ISBN 978-1-943959-24-2
© 2017 Kelsey Norman

The Team: Miralee Ferrell, Nikki Wright, Cindy Jackson, Donita K. Paul
Cover Design: Indie Cover Design, Lynnette Bonner Designer

Mountain Brook Ink is an inspirational publisher offering fiction you can believe in.
Printed in the United States of America

DEDICATION

To my sweet daughter. You are a light in this dark world.

ACKNOWLEDGMENTS

I would like to thank the following people:

- My husband, Joel Norman, for being my best friend through everything.

- My family, for being supportive and encouraging through my writing journey and challenges.

- Donita K. Paul, for doing an awesome content edit.

- Miralee Ferrell, for being an understanding publisher and friend.

- Everyone who did reviews and spread the word about my novels.

- And most importantly, my Lord and Savior.

CHAPTER ONE

SMALL CLOUDS TOOK SHAPE IN FRONT of my lips and slowly drifted away. My fingers stiffened as I cinched Hezzie's saddle. His big, glassy eyes seemed to beg me to not take him for a ride.

"Sorry, buddy, it's happening," I said, patting my favorite horse's neck.

With an exasperated sigh, Hezzie glanced at Hazel with apparent envy. The temperamental mare looked warm and comfortable in her pen.

"Come on, the exercise will be good for you." I grabbed Hezzie's reins and led him out of the stable.

The biting wind cut right through my coat and chilled me to my bones. Winter was fast approaching, which meant night fell much earlier than I was accustomed. The sun was beginning its descent creating streaks of orange and purple in the cloudy sky.

"We're going to be late," I said, placing my left foot in a stirrup. I did a quick hop and plopped into the saddle. Before gripping the reins, I slid my icy fingers into my gloves and tugged on my stocking cap. I clicked my tongue, summoning Hezzie to start at a slow trot.

We passed my grandparents' little, white farmhouse where smoke snaked out of the chimney. I imagined Papa stoking the flames in the fireplace and Grams working her fingers raw in the kitchen. A smidgen of guilt crawled through my mind. I should have been in there helping my grandparents since they'd done so much for me recently. But my heart didn't agree—my heart pushed me to ride like the wind toward the clearing.

Hezzie increased his speed when we reached the wheat field.

Harvest and the changing of the seasons had left the vast fields dry and bleak. However, in a couple of months, green buds would start breaking through the soil and eventually the golden sea would return. It was amazing how even under harsh conditions life could begin fresh. But wasn't I a testament to that? The man I'd thought I loved had nearly killed me twice, yet I'd been able to recover and start a new life.

Thank you, God, for allowing me to live another day.

I dug my heels into Hezzie's sides, encouraging him to take off in a canter. It wasn't long before the thick row of trees separating my grandparents' and the Nelsons' property came into view. My heart raced in anticipation as Hezzie slowed then came to a stop in front of the cluster of trees.

Almost all the leaves had fallen from the branches. The stubborn ones that remained were barely hanging on. Even though the trees were nearly naked, I still couldn't see through to the other side.

I dismounted and pulled off my hat, tucking it into my coat pocket. I ran my fingers through my static-filled hair. For the past month, I hadn't missed one of these visits, yet I still got nervous. What if one day he wasn't here? What if at some point he was no longer allowed to visit?

With a quick breath, I ducked and twisted through the branches. The fallen leaves crunched beneath my cowboy boots. The clearing I stepped into held dead grass and patches of dirt. A small pond sat in the middle with a thin sheet of ice covering the top.

I pulled up the sleeve of my coat and glanced at my watch. *He should be here by now.* Had something happened? What if he'd been detained in his world? Worry niggled at my mind. He'd never been late before. After losing him not long ago, I wasn't sure I could go through something like that again.

A sudden gust of wind made the surrounding trees creak and sway. The tension at the nape of my neck eased. I smiled. Those blasts of air were a signal that in a matter of seconds I'd be in his arms.

I watched in awe as his presence made the brown grass at my feet change to a deep green. Daisies and unrecognizable flowers wound their way up through the soil. The temperature still felt like winter, but I was surrounded by summer.

Strong arms suddenly banded around me from behind. Firm lips grazed my cheek. I closed my eyes and inhaled deeply, soaking up the smell of honeysuckle coming from his skin.

"You're late," I said.

"By thirty seconds," Liam said at my ear.

I turned to face him. My heart stuttered. I still couldn't get over how handsome he was with those dark brown eyes, chiseled jaw, and gorgeous grin. I wrapped my arms around his waist and dropped my head back to look into his eyes. "That's thirty seconds lost out of the measly two hours that we have to be together."

"I'm sorry. It won't happen again." He leaned down, nuzzling my neck with his nose. "How can I make it up to you?"

My breath fell short. "I'm sure you can find a way."

His lips were on mine then. I draped my arms around his shoulders, coiling my fingers through his long, black hair. When he pulled away, I felt dizzy.

"Forgive me now?"

"Yes," I squeaked.

Liam laughed as he pulled me down to sit with him in the thick grass. I rested my back against his chest, welcoming his warmth. He wrapped his bare arms around my middle. "You're shivering," he said, tightening his hold.

"I think you forget that I'm human. I'm not impervious to temperatures like you."

"I never forget that you're human," he said firmly.

Neither did I. And I never forgot that he wasn't. Which was why we had this limited time together. When Liam was assigned as my Martyr so many months ago, I thought he'd complete the unknown task he'd been sent to do, and then return to the mysterious place he'd come from. But over the duration of his stay, I fell in love. It wasn't his supernatural abilities, his gorgeous looks, or his need to protect me that made me fall. It was him. I loved *him*.

Liam treated me with the respect I always wanted but never received from my abusive ex-boyfriend, Jeremy. Jeremy had made me feel I wasn't worthy of love. Liam helped me to realize that I was. Even though Liam could easily overpower me, he was good and gentle. And he loved with a selflessness that could only come from somebody not of this world.

It was torture only being able to see him a couple of hours a day. And it wasn't fair that he couldn't leave the clearing. I should have been happy that he was able to come back to Earth at all, but sometimes it wasn't enough.

"You're thinking it again," Liam said.

I craned my neck to look at him. "Are you using your mind-reading ability on me, or am I that transparent?"

His mouth shifted to the side. "Both."

I released a long sigh. "Sorry. I can't help it."

Liam kissed my temple. "Our relationship isn't exactly normal, is it?"

I snorted. "That's putting it mildly. I've never heard of a relationship between another human and an immortal." I breathed out a laugh. "Then again, I didn't know immortals existed until I met you."

"I recently learned of a similar relationship."

My brows wrinkled. "Another Martyr and human fell in love?"

"Yes."

"Are they still together?"

The corners of Liam's mouth dropped slightly. "No."

My heart jumped. "What happened?"

"I'm not sure I should tell you the story."

"Why not?"

"It doesn't have a happy ending."

I turned my body around, sitting cross-legged in front of him. "I can take it."

"All right." He rubbed at the cleft in his chin. "Fifty years ago, a Martyr christened Julian fell in love with his assignment, Hattie. They knew that once his assignment was complete, a relationship would be impossible. So Julian chose to become mortal."

My eyes widened. "I thought you said there isn't a way for you to become human."

"There is, but there are consequences."

"What kind of consequences?"

"In order for a Martyr to become mortal, he or she must find a Rogue."

"What's a Rogue?"

Liam's hands fisted. "They inhabit the souls of people who have wicked hearts and force them to commit evil acts."

A shudder crawled up my spine. Martyrs . . . Rogues . . . were there other immortals who roamed our world? Dozens of other questions invaded my mind, but they'd have to wait.

"So Julian found a Rogue?"

"Yes. He had to promise his soul to them. Any Rogue would be able to use his body to carry out their crimes."

"He agreed to this?"

Liam nodded.

"What did Hattie think about the agreement?"

"She didn't know."

I raised my brows. "He didn't tell her?"

Liam shook his head slowly.

"So what happened?"

"They lived happily for a time. It was two years before the first Rogue came."

"What did the Rogue make him do?"

"He assaulted a homeless man."

Another shudder. "Why would they make him do that?"

"Because they could."

5

How cruel. To take over somebody's mind and body to do your bidding.

"It wasn't long after that another Rogue came. Eventually the acts became more violent. Until . . ." Liam glanced down at his hands, clenching and unclenching.

"Until what?"

His eyes met mine. "Julian hurt Hattie."

Tears stung my eyes. I knew all too well what it was like to be harmed by somebody you thought loved you. "Did he kill her?"

Liam shook his head. "Thankfully, no. Julian tried to explain that it hadn't been him, but Hattie didn't believe him. So she left."

"What happened to Julian?"

"Without Hattie, he felt his life on Earth no longer held any significance. He sought out Rogues, begging them to use him. He did unspeakable things. In the end, he was caught by authorities and judged for his crimes. He spent the remainder of his life in prison."

My eyes filled with tears.

"After what happened with Julian, the two-hour regulation was established to prevent other Martyrs from making the same decision."

A tear rolled down my cheek. Liam wiped at it with the pad of his thumb.

"We aren't told the visitation rule unless we request access to Earth once our assignment is complete. It's preferred we don't return. We don't want to risk our true identities being revealed."

"To who? Humans?"

"And Rogues."

"Why?"

"Rogues would do anything to possess a Martyr's soul."

I wrapped my arms around myself to conceal another shiver. As much as I loved the idea of Liam being able to be with me without any restrictions, I didn't like that his soul wouldn't be his own. It all sounded too much like spiritual warfare to me—like he'd have to give his life to Satan. A shudder ran through me. That was unthinkable. Surely, he wouldn't give up his soul only so he could be with me.

I cleared my throat. "Have you ever considered approaching a Rogue? To become mortal?" The wind blew a lock of hair across Liam's face. He shoved it behind his ear. "Yes, but I never would."

My shoulders sagged with an overwhelming sense of relief. I cupped his cheeks. "Good. I wouldn't let you do it anyway." I pulled him to me, pressing my lips to his once again.

LIAM COULDN'T GET ENOUGH of Nina. When he kissed her, he felt her soul. Her fears, her passions, her sorrows, her joys . . . he experienced them all. With each kiss, a piece of her became a part of him.

Liam broke the kiss and brushed Nina's auburn hair from her forehead. She was so beautiful. He would do anything to be with this woman he adored.

He had seriously considered finding a Rogue. He'd weighed the consequences against the benefits but came to his senses when he realized the price. There was no way he could risk hurting Nina. Besides, he wouldn't truly be human if his soul belonged to the Rogues.

The moment he first saw Nina, something in him awakened. Nothing else seemed to matter except her.

It was here at the pond that he had first encountered her. He'd unintentionally frightened Nina, yet those green eyes of hers had still held such strength and tenacity. When his gaze had landed on the scar at her neck, her thoughts flooded his mind, and he saw who had marred her skin and spirit. The pain Liam felt when he healed wounds paled in comparison to the agony Nina had experienced at the hands of Jeremy.

"What are you thinking about?" Nina asked.

"How brave and strong you are."

She blushed and dipped her head.

She didn't know how courageous she truly was. To have suffered as she had and still come out of it showed true perseverance. She was still tortured by the memories of her past, but each day seemed to get easier.

"Did you have a nightmare last night?" Liam asked.

Nina released a sigh. "Sort of."

"What do you mean?"

She lifted her eyes to meet his gaze. "It wasn't like the ones I usually have. It wasn't a memory of Jeremy."

"What was it?"

"There was a strange man present." Her body trembled. Whether from the cold or from the memory, Liam couldn't tell.

He slid his arm around her waist. "Who was he?"

"I don't know. I never saw his face. He wore all black with a hood over his head."

Liam's heart suddenly beat faster. "Did he say anything?"

Nina shook her head. "He stood off to the side, watching me as the dream played out."

Liam swallowed hard and tried to stay relaxed. Nina would notice if he allowed himself to stiffen or he showed too much concern. And he didn't want to frighten her.

For humans, dreams often meant nothing. They were images seen on TV, ideas read about in books, or a replay of events that had occurred during the day. They held no true significance.

But for a Martyr, a dream was an omen. And it shouldn't be ignored.

CHAPTER TWO

OUR DAILY TIME TOGETHER WAS NEARING an end. The wind had increased, bringing along with it a chill that made my teeth chatter. I wrapped my coat closer and tried to hide my shiver. If Liam knew how cold I was, he would probably start cutting our time short or decide we should only see each other on warm days.

"What are we going to do once winter hits full force? You're going to freeze out here," Liam said, lifting me with him to stand.

So much for trying to conceal my shudder. "I'll wear two coats. Or skin a bear and wear its fur."

He gave me a crooked grin. "They don't have bears in Kansas."

"I'll figure out something. Not even a blizzard could keep me away from you."

Liam pulled my stocking cap from my coat pocket and tugged it on over my head. "What if you get frost bite? Or hypothermia?"

I hugged him to me. "If that happens, then you can heal me."

He tipped my chin. "Is that the only reason you visit? So I can heal your ailments?"

"No, there are other reasons, too."

He flashed that amazing smile he reserved only for me in these sweet moments. "And they are?"

"You can probably figure them out."

"Is this one?" He bent his head and kissed me softly.

Warmth shot through my body. When he pulled away, my cheeks flushed. "Yes. One of the many."

Liam wrapped his arms around me in a tight embrace. "It's time," he said into my hair.

As usual, my heartbeat increased at the thought of leaving him yet again. I groaned and moved away, putting a few feet of space between us. It was always easier to say goodbye if we weren't touching.

"I love you," he said.

"I love you." I bit my lip as tears stung my eyes. What if this was the last time I ever saw him?

"It's not the last time, Nina."

I squinted. "You're not supposed to do that." How could he remain so calm when we couldn't be together? But I had to admit, his attempt at cheering me up had worked. His smile alone made me forgive him.

"See you tomorrow," Liam said.

I pointed at him. "You better be on time."

He straightened, raised his arm, and mocked a brief salute. "Yes, ma'am. Sleep well."

With a quick wave, I stepped through to the other side of the trees. Hopefully the next twenty-two hours would fly by.

AFTER MAKING SURE HEZZIE was warm and settled in his pen, I ran to the farmhouse. The back door slammed behind me as I walked into the kitchen.

Grams spun around from the stove, tossing her long gray braid over her shoulder. She glanced at me over the top of her glasses. "You won't be able to do these night rides much longer. The weather man said we're in for a frigid winter."

I shrugged out of my coat. "I can hack it. New York didn't exactly have warm winters." I leaned against the counter, peering into the pot on the stove. "What are you making?"

Grams released a long sigh. "Pudding."

"Again? Has Papa eaten anything else since Monday?"

She shook her head slowly.

Papa had had another round of chemotherapy a few days ago. The treatments left him weak and sick for days afterward. Prostate cancer was said to have a high remission rate. Papa's tumor had spread to the tissue surrounding the prostate, but his oncologist felt confident that the chemo was working to prevent it from spreading any further.

With a pat on Grams' arm, I headed into the living room. I found Papa watching the news from his recliner. Since losing so much weight, his leathery skin seemed to hang off his body.

Please, God, let him come through this.

He must have felt me staring as he turned in my direction. He shot me a frail smile. "Hey, sweet pea."

I pasted on a grin and plopped onto the sofa. "Hey, Papa. How are you?"

"Getting by. How was your ride?"

"Cold."

"Where do you go during these evening rides?"

I shifted my gaze, picking at the lint from the afghan draped across the couch. "All over. Nowhere in particular." He knew I was lying. I could sense it.

Papa was there that night four months ago. The night my psycho ex tracked me down to finish the job he'd begun a couple of months before. He'd almost succeeded, until Liam literally transferred my bullet wound to himself.

And Papa had witnessed it all. Yet we still had never talked about it. Why couldn't I tell him? I trusted him to keep my secret. But would he even believe me? I'd never known Martyrs existed until Liam came along. Did Papa believe in the supernatural? Surely he did after what he'd seen that night.

"Nina..."

This is it. He's going to probe for information. I took a deep breath and looked at him.

Papa squinted at me. Was he afraid to ask? Maybe he didn't know how. Or maybe he was like I was in the beginning and the idea that immortals existed was too much to grasp.

The television suddenly blared loud instrumental music. Papa and I jerked our heads toward the screen. A female newscaster sitting behind a desk seemed to stare directly at us as the words *Breaking News* scrolled across the bottom of the screen.

"Two people are dead this evening after a Beloit man shot his wife before turning the gun on himself. Neighbors say they are shocked," the anchor said.

The screen switched to a different woman standing outside in a residential neighborhood. An ambulance and police lights flashed behind her on a darkened street. "Tim was always such a nice guy. I don't get it. Something in him must have snapped."

The newscaster returned. "Police say the man had a clean record, and they are currently seeking a motive." She glanced at her notes. "In other breaking news, a Beloit woman is in the hospital after an intruder broke into her home, raped her, and left her for dead."

Beloit was only an hour away. Crimes like these seemed to happen frequently in New York City, but I never expected them in rural Kansas.

Papa snatched the remote and turned off the television. "This world has gone to hell." He sighed and rubbed his hand over his bald head.

I knotted my fingers around the afghan. *Is he going to ask me now?*

"Do you work tomorrow?" he asked.

Not the question I expected. I nodded. "Noon to five."

"You liking it so far?"

I shrugged. "It's all right."

It had been a week since I'd taken a job as a bank teller at the only bank in the tiny town of Despair. Being twenty-five years old, I realized I couldn't live with my grandparents forever. It was time to start saving money so that I could get my own place. I didn't know where I'd live, but it had to be somewhere close so I could visit Liam. I smacked my hands on my thighs and stood. "Well, I'm off to bed." I kissed Papa on the forehead. "Good night." With a sigh of relief, I shuffled to my bedroom. I was able to dodge Papa's questions this time, but for how much longer?

Like every evening, my body was drained to the point that I barely had enough energy to change my clothes. Somehow I found one last bit of strength to put on my pajama pants and a T-shirt. I collapsed onto the bed, my eyes closing as soon as my head hit the pillow. But as always, my mind wouldn't shut down, and the continuous nightly war raged between my brain and body.

Tonight's replay of events included the story Liam had told me. A tremor shook my body as I thought back to the disturbing details. I couldn't imagine somebody taking over my soul and having no control over my actions.

How did Rogues inhabit human souls anyway? What did Rogues look like? Had I ever encountered a Rogue and didn't know it? Question after question bombarded my mind. Hopefully Liam would be able to answer them tomorrow.

I rolled over to my side and stared out the window. The sky looked like a dark abyss about to swallow the world whole. Was Liam up there somewhere? What was he doing at that moment? Was he thinking about me? Did he have a physical form when he went home? Or was he merely a spirit without a body? I didn't like not knowing—I wanted to understand more about this man I'd grown to love. It had taken time for me to trust again after the terror I'd endured with Jeremy, but now that I'd given my heart, there was so much I longed to know.

If Papa ever did ask me for the truth about Liam, there wasn't much I could tell him. Where he came from or anything dealing with the existence of Martyrs were questions *I* didn't even have the answers to.

I closed my eyes and thought of Liam until eventually I drifted off.

I STOOD IN A never-ending, narrow hallway with bare, purple walls. No sounds bounced off the walls. No smells permeated the room. And there were no signs of life other than my own.

I glanced down at the floor. A pane of glass separated me from the vines slithering along the underside. Wait a minute. Those weren't vines. I bent over to get a better look.

Snakes! My heart jumped and a shriek passed my lips. The scream echoed through the hall in different pitches. With a deep breath, I closed my eyes. I opened them slowly and looked up to find the ceiling absent. Instead, grey clouds swirled overhead. I narrowed my eyes. Were they creating faces? One of the clouds contorted into a fanged beast with beady eyes and pointed horns. The ghastly thing stared right at me.

A shiver crawled up my spine, and I turned my gaze away, scanning the no longer vacant walls. To the left, painted portraits hung in disarray. To my right were perfectly aligned mirrors of different shapes and sizes.

I approached a large mirror in the shape of a triangle. My reflection wasn't present. I held out my hands in front of my face. They were visible to my own eyes, so why didn't they show up in the mirror?

Strange. I stretched my fingers out toward the glass of the mirror.

"Don't!" a small voice cried behind me.

I jerked my hand away and spun around. Had that come from the painting?

A little boy with black hair stared directly at me. I took

tentative steps toward the painting until I was almost nose to nose with the boy. His brown eyes drooped while his mouth curved into a frown. Why was he sad?

He blinked.

I gasped and pulled my head back.

His eyes widened, and he tilted his head to peer around me.

"Nina," a deep voice hissed at my ear. I whirled around. My reflection suddenly existed in the triangle mirror. Only it didn't look exactly like me. I wore a gorgeous purple gown, and my hair was a beautiful shade of red and full of volume. My green eyes were larger and seemed to sparkle. Something else was different, but what was it? The scar! It was gone.

I reached up to touch my throat. My reflection did not. I took a step toward the woman who was not me. She was so beautiful.

"Don't!" the boy from the painting called.

I ignored him and reached for the mirror once again. My non-reflection smiled with rosy lips. My own lips pulled into a smile. I wanted to know this woman in the mirror. She seemed so alive. So happy.

She was suddenly gone. *No! Come back!*

Blue fog took her place, swirling behind the mirror. A figure slowly glided through it. I narrowed my eyes to get a better look. A man in dark clothing stealthily creeped toward me.

"Run!" the painting boy cried.

I ignored him still. I had to know who this was in the mirror.

The cloaked figure kept his head down. A black hood cast a shadow over his face. If only he would look up. Then I could see who he was.

As though he read my mind, he slowly lifted his head. My heart leapt into my throat.

Jeremy.

No. It couldn't be. Why was he here? I thought I'd never see him again. Panic rose in my chest and I wanted to dart away, but something kept me planted in place. I didn't want to look at him, but it was as though I had no control over my actions. My gaze took him in.

His pallid skin appeared soft as a rose petal. My fingers twitched, aching to stroke his cheek. His usual bright, blue eyes had faded to the color of ice. His pale lips turned up into a small smile. Despite his frightening appearance, he was still so handsome.

I shook my head. Wait, what was I thinking? This man wasn't handsome. He was vile.

His smile suddenly widened until he revealed his teeth. They seemed straighter. More white than before. I found my own mouth twitching into a smile.

Without warning, his gloved hand shot out of the mirror and wrapped around my throat.

CHAPTER THREE

WITH A CHOKED BREATH, I SHOT out of bed and clutched at my neck.

"It was a dream. Only a dream," I whispered to the night. I wrapped my arms around myself and raked in sharp breaths as my heartrate slowed. Once my lungs could easily fill with air, I fisted my hands and beat them on my temples. "Get out of my head."

Why couldn't I seem to let my past go? Had the years of abuse made it impossible? My gut coiled, and I clutched my stomach. Would I be haunted by the memories of Jeremy for the rest of my life?

I threw myself back on the pillow and gazed unseeingly at the ceiling fan above my bed, trying to not think about the dream, but failing.

What had it meant? Surely it was only a dream. Nothing more. Jeremy was dead. He'd been dead for months. I saw his lifeless body lying in a mud puddle after Liam had broken his neck. I watched the EMT's cover him with a white sheet and carry him away.

What had they done with his body? Was there a funeral? Did they bury him?

I gritted my teeth and draped my arms over my eyes. It was going to be a very long day. I would have to force myself to stay awake the rest of the night. There was no way I'd let the frightening nightmare continue.

With a sigh, I rolled over to my side to watch the sun rise as

I prayed.

MY GRANDPARENTS' TRUCK, OLD Blue, hated the cold as much as I did. It coughed and wheezed as I drove along the country road leading to Despair. I was on my way to work and only a few miles from home when the truck gave up and died in the middle of the road.

"Come on," I mumbled as I turned the key.

The engine sputtered but still didn't start. The poor truck didn't have much life left. I'd probably need to buy a car before I tried to get my own place.

Maybe Old Blue needed a few minutes to recharge. I released the key and rested my head against the driver's seat. I shivered as I stared out the windshield. The day had started out sunny, now dark clouds swirled in the sky. I was beginning to believe what the locals said about Kansas weather being fickle. Papa said that in the winter it's even worse. One day it could be sixty degrees and within twenty-four hours it could snow.

At that moment, small white flakes slowly drifted down to land on the windshield. "Great," I said on a sigh.

I grabbed hold of the key and turned it in the ignition. Still nothing. The engine didn't even make a noise. I mashed my lips together and punched the steering wheel. Fantastic. I was going to be late to work. If I couldn't get it to start, then I'd have to walk home. Despair was too far away. The snow barely fell, but walking in it for another seven miles didn't sound appealing.

I tucked my chin into my coat and yawned. Movement in the driver's side mirror caught my eye. I leaned forward to get a better look. A person walked down the middle of the road in my direction. They were too far away to discern much about them, but I could tell they had the gait of a man. Maybe he could help get the truck started. What was he doing out here? Did his car break down as well?

I turned around, glancing through the back window. The man was no longer there. I scanned the surrounding fields. Nothing but cows.

Weird.

I faced forward, looking to the side mirror. Wait a minute, there he was. And he was even closer than before. I squinted. Definitely a man, but the hood of his black jacket concealed his face.

Spinning around, I looked behind me once more. Nothing. I pinched the bridge of my nose. *Get a grip, Nina.* Insomnia could do strange things to a person. I really needed to get some sleep.

I turned back around, glancing in the mirror. All clear. I grabbed hold of the key in the ignition and prayed the truck would start. It slowly rumbled to life. The tires kicked up gravel as I sped down the road.

OLD BLUE CLUNKED DOWN the short main drag of Despair. I stopped at the only stoplight, watching the snowflakes blanket the pot-holed road. When the light turned green, I eased my way down the street, glancing at the small businesses on either side. Each storefront could use a major facelift, but the people of Despair weren't much for flash. The saying "if it ain't broke, don't fix it" could be the town motto.

The street was deserted. Even the parking lot of the grocery store was bare. Perhaps when it snowed around here people hunkered down to wait it out. It wasn't that way back in New York. The sky could be falling and people would still be out and about.

Within seconds, I reached the end of the street and pulled

into the parking lot behind Farmers National Bank and Trust. The bank had once been a used car dealership. Therefore, large windows encased most of the building. It didn't seem very safe for a bank, but at least I had a clear view of Main Street from the teller counter. Not that anything exciting ever went by.

I hopped out of the truck and entered the building through the back door. When I reached the lobby, the snow had already stopped, leaving behind a thin layer of white dust. Pity. Watching the flakes fall would have been the highlight of my day.

My co-worker sat at the counter, texting away on her phone.

"Good morning, Kaley," I said as I hung my coat on the hall tree.

She didn't look at me as she barely murmured a hello. Kaley had recently graduated from high school and was taking a year to earn money for college. She was a sweet girl, but extremely quiet. Our conversations were usually one-sided.

I sat on my stool and glanced at her fingers moving rapidly across the screen of her phone. I didn't think I'd need a cell phone ever again since the only people who needed to contact me were my grandparents and Liam, but after the fiasco with the truck, it'd probably be a good idea to get one.

"Do you like your smartphone?" I asked Kaley.

"Uh-huh."

"Who are you texting?"

"My boyfriend."

My brows shot up. "You have a boyfriend? I didn't know that."

No response.

I'd never been very good at making friends. In high school I was socially awkward and preferred hanging out with my dad. At twenty, I started dating Jeremy, which made most women hate me. I never understood it. Was it because I was with somebody they wanted? Sadly, most of them had been with him behind my back.

This summer I'd started to develop a friendship with our neighbor Ruthie Nelson, but after what happened at her house with Jeremy and her daughter Lulu almost getting killed, we hadn't talked much. All I really had were my grandparents and Liam—an old married couple, and an immortal man I could only see two hours a day. What great company I kept.

I released a loud sigh and rested my chin in my hand. The day was moving way too slow and I still had a few hours left of work. Idleness wasn't good for my sleep-deprived mind and body. My eyelids started to droop when the bell above the entrance dinged, indicating we had a customer.

I straightened and blinked a few times. When I saw who was walking toward me, my stomach dropped.

Oh no, not Creepy Carl. I'd first met him this summer when he'd hit on me at the Farmers' market, then encountered him again at the Fourth of July carnival. Those two interactions were enough for a lifetime.

Carl rested his plump arm on the counter and leaned against it. He flashed me a wide grin with missing teeth and rotted stubs.

I leaned away. Ugh, he smelled like he'd bathed in vinegar. I swallowed back a gag and resisted the urge to pinch my nose.

"Look who we have here. How ya doin', Nina?" he slurred over the wad of tobacco tucked under his lower lip.

"Good afternoon," I said through a tight throat as I tried to hold my breath. "What can I do for you?"

He raked his fingers through his greasy hair. "Well, since you asked, I'll take a date."

My eyes narrowed. "I meant what can I do for you in terms of banking?"

"We'll get to that. Can I take you out?"

"I have a boyfriend."

"Rumor is that he disappeared after what happened at the Nelsons'."

He didn't know how right he was.

21

I cleared my throat. "You heard wrong. Now, deposit or withdraw?"

Carl closed his eyes and sucked in a breath so deep that his chest expanded to the point I thought it would burst. When he opened his eyes, his pupils dilated. I couldn't even see the color of his irises.

Goosebumps sprouted on my arms. Something was off about him. More so than usual.

Carl's smirk disappeared. "Withdraw," he said in a deeper than normal voice.

Somebody didn't take rejection well.

I shifted to stand in front of the computer. "What's your account number?" I stared at the computer screen. Anything to not have to look at him.

"Um, Nina," Kaley said with a shaky voice.

I looked in her direction. Her eyes were wide, her hands trembling.

Swallowing hard, I turned my attention back to Carl. My heart dropped into my stomach. I stared right down the barrel of a hand gun.

Please, God, not again.

"Give me all the money you have in your drawer," Carl said calmly.

I couldn't move. I couldn't breathe.

The hammer of the gun clicked. "Now!"

His tone of voice made me nearly jump out of my skin. I blinked and was suddenly able to move. My hands trembled as they hovered over the computer keyboard. What was my password? Why wouldn't my fingers cooperate?

"Don't you dare hit that button," he said, pointing the gun at Kaley.

Kaley's hand stopped on its way to the emergency switch beneath the counter. She stiffened as tears ran down her cheeks.

With my heart pounding in my chest, I moved in front of the

gun and stared Carl down. Sweat trailed over his left eyebrow and into his eye. He didn't even blink.

What was going on? He'd always made me feel uneasy, but I never expected him to do something like this. With an unsteady breath, I typed in the password to open my drawer. The drawer popped open.

Carl kept the gun trained on me as he pulled a plastic sack from his pocket and slapped it on the counter. "Put it in." As I placed the money in the bag, all I could think was how unlucky I was. This was the second time within four months that I'd had a gun pointed at me. Was I a magnet for violence?

"Now her drawer."

I slid over in front of Kaley who hadn't moved an inch. When all the money from that drawer was in the bag, Carl snatched it and flung it over his shoulder. He kept his gaze and the gun trained on me.

My heart hammered as sweat trickled down my spine. What now? Would he kill us? Surely he realized that I'd be able to give the police his name.

Kaley sobbed softly behind me. I reached back, clutching her hand. She squeezed it in a death grip.

"Both of you turn around," Carl growled.

With a deep breath, I turned slowly as I continued to hold Kaley's hand. She turned as well, her sobs growing louder.

A tear rolled down my cheek as I closed my eyes. It was hard to believe that after all I'd lived through, this was how I was going to die. I thought God wasn't done with me yet. I was finally starting to feel like He wasn't punishing me for turning away from my faith. Maybe I was wrong.

I didn't think about the pain that was sure to come. All I could think about was Liam. He would go to the clearing tonight and I wouldn't be there. Would he panic? Would he try to get out and find me? And what about Grams and Papa? Hadn't they been through enough already?

More tears seeped from the corners of my eyes.

Kaley and I waited. And waited. But nothing happened.

The vinegar odor suddenly disappeared. I glanced over my shoulder. Carl had vanished as well.

I spun around, peering out the large windows. The street and sidewalk were still empty. Kaley and I were the only ones in the bank, therefore the only witnesses. Other than the empty registers, no damage had been done. And no evidence had been left behind. It was as though nothing had happened. Thankfully, the security cameras would be able to prove that it had.

I turned back around and placed a hand on Kaley's shoulder. "He's gone, Kaley. We're safe."

With a sigh of relief, she pulled me into a hug and continued to weep into my shoulder.

I choked on my own sob as I held onto her.

CHAPTER FOUR

LIAM PACED THE CLEARING AND STABBED his fingers through his hair. Nina was never late. What if she was in trouble?

His right hand fisted, and he beat it against the invisible wall that surrounded the clearing. With the force he put behind the punch, an ordinary wall would have crumbled to dust. This wall barely rippled. He knew he wouldn't be able to get past it—one more stipulation for being able to visit Nina.

He felt like a caged animal. He wanted to be free. Free to roam the earth as he pleased and to be with the woman he loved. He wanted to be human. But he couldn't. Even if surrendering his soul to the Rogues wasn't a factor, would he be able to give up what he was created for? Being a Martyr was his life's purpose.

With a sigh, Liam plopped down in the grass. He stared at the section of trees that Nina usually entered through, willing her to appear.

"Come on, Nina," he whispered.

He couldn't protect her from in here. If anything ever happened to her, he'd never be able to forgive himself. Perhaps he should call on a Rogue after all. Maybe he'd be strong enough to resist their power.

It would be simple. All he'd have to do is say aloud the words he was warned never to utter, and a Rogue would find him.

I'm ready to give myself up. My soul is yours. Come to me. Even just thinking the words caused him to shudder.

How long would it take for a Rogue to find him? Hours? Days? Could he be with Nina freely in a matter of minutes?

Liam's lips parted and for a moment he considered saying the words. He closed his eyes and shook his head. Was he going mad? There was no way he could give his soul to one of those monsters.

A breeze swept through the clearing, bringing with it Nina's scent—sunshine and jasmine. He'd recognize that fragrance anywhere. The thoughts he'd had moments ago disappeared and Liam sprung to his feet. He felt her before he saw her. A smile spread across his face but disappeared as she stepped through the trees.

Her green eyes were dilated as though in shock. She met his gaze, and her chin trembled. He was in front of her in half a second, draping her in a hug. She wrapped her arms around his waist, sobbing into his chest.

Her fragmented thoughts whispered across his mind. *Bank. Robbed. Gun.*

Liam pulled away, scanning her for injuries. She looked unharmed. Her cries turned to hiccups, until she was hyperventilating.

Liam grabbed hold of her face, forcing her to look at him. Her bloodshot eyes couldn't focus. He projected his calm onto her, trying to ease her anxiety. Nina continued to weep uncontrollably. She was too distraught to calm with his usual methods. It was time for a more drastic measure.

Liam ran his hand down her face from forehead to chin. She fell limp in his arms.

MY EYES FLUTTERED OPEN and honeysuckle wafted up my nose. Snuggled against Liam's chest was the best place to wake up. But I didn't want him to know I was awake. Not yet anyway. I'd only have to talk about what had happened. And I didn't want to remember.

"I need you to tell me," Liam whispered.

How did he know I was awake?

"Your breathing changed. And you instantly began thinking."

I leaned away so I could look at him. "We may need to revisit that rule we made about you not listening to my thoughts unless absolutely necessary."

He smiled. "I think this qualifies."

"I'm sorry I'm late."

Liam's arms tightened around me. "What happened?"

"I was talking with the police. Creepy Carl robbed the bank."

His brows wrinkled. "That man I met at the carnival?"

"Yes."

"Does he have a record?"

"No. The police were shocked that he would do something like this."

"Did they catch him?"

I shook my head. "They're looking."

Liam sighed. "Are you okay?"

My chin quivered as I thought back to the gun pointed directly at me. Why hadn't Carl pulled the trigger? I was so sure I was going to die.

A muscle in Liam's jaw ticked. "Tell me everything." With a deep breath, I recounted the same statement I'd given the police. I'd told the story to so many different officials, that telling it again felt rehearsed. I paused when I got to the part where Carl had told me and Kaley to turn around.

A tear rolled down my cheek. "I waited for the pain to come, but it never did. It wasn't until the smell of vinegar disappeared that I knew he was gone."

Liam's eyes widened. "Vinegar? He smelled like vinegar?"

My brows wrinkled. "Yes. Why?"

Liam grabbed my shoulders, shifting me to face him. Was

that   panic   in   his   eyes?
"What else, Nina? Did you notice anything else strange about
Carl? Anything about his eyes?"

A small jolt of shock raced through me as I remembered
Carl's eyes and the wild look within them. "Yes, actually, they
dilated   right   before   he   pulled   the   gun."
Liam closed his eyes and shook his head.

My heart pounded. What was going on? "You're scaring me.
What's wrong?"

He opened his eyes and gave me a swift kiss on the forehead.
"I have to go," he said, coming to his feet.

I scrambled to my own. "But we still have time left."

He pinched the bridge of his nose. "I know. I don't want to
leave, but I have to. I need to report this."

"Report what? To who?" I grabbed his hand. It was shaking.
"Liam, what's going on?"

"Do you work tomorrow?"

"Yes, but—"

He cupped my cheeks. "Promise me you won't leave the
farm tomorrow. Please?"

I didn't know what had this strong man so frightened, but I
trusted him, and if he didn't want me to go to work then I
wouldn't.

"I promise."

Liam pressed his lips to mine, kissing me as though it was
our last. When I opened my eyes, he was gone.

For an hour, I paced around the pond as I waited for Liam to
return. He didn't.

What could have been so important that he'd leave? Why
was he so concerned with the fact that Carl had smelled like
vinegar and his eyes dilated?

I stopped, my eyes widening. Wait a second. Carl acted out
of character by committing a crime. His demeanor and
appearance had changed unexpectedly. He couldn't have been

taken over by a Rogue, could he?

I shook my head. No, the thought was silly. There had to be another explanation.

I glanced around the clearing once more. Looked like Liam wasn't coming back tonight. With my shoulders slumped, I headed back through the trees and hopped onto Hezzie's back. On the ride to the stable, Hezzie kept trying to take off to get out of the cold. I forced him to stay at a slow trot. Returning home would only mean I'd have to be under the scrutiny of my grandparents.

After contacting the police, I'd called Grams and Papa. They were panicked and in disbelief that Carl would do such a thing. They'd both known him since he was a boy. Last year when Carl had approached me at the farmers' market, Grams had said he was harmless. It only proved that you never knew what somebody was capable of, no matter how well you thought you knew them.

When I got home after work, my grandparents had swarmed me with their embraces, but all I'd wanted to do was get to Liam. Too much of our precious time together had already been wasted. Grams and Papa had begged me not to go on my nightly ride. I told them it was the only thing that could calm me down, and they reluctantly allowed me to go.

I couldn't help but feel guilty. I'd caused them so much worry since moving here. Ashamed of my relationship with Jeremy, I hadn't included my grandparents in my life for years. It wasn't until the first time he almost killed me that I reached out to them. They had welcomed me with open arms, not once chastising me for shutting them out.

Those first couple of months, they endured waking me from my night terrors and trying to get me to eat, all while working to get to know me again. Then, the unthinkable happened. After Jeremy was released from prison, he came after me. Once again, he tried to kill me, and my grandparents were there to help me through the aftermath, at the same time they dealt with Papa's cancer.

Chaos seemed to follow me no matter where I went or what I did. Grams and Papa had been caught in the cross hairs more than enough. Maybe it would be better if I left.

A tear trailed down my cheek as I gazed at the starry sky. "Lord, I don't know what to do. I'm tired of hurting the people I love." My prayer cut off with a sob.

I TOOK A DEEP breath and wiped at my eyes before walking into the house. Minnie, the fat farm cat, appeared out of the shadows and sauntered onto the back porch. She rubbed against my leg with a meow.

My impulse was to shoo her away, but instead I stooped and scratched her under her chin. She purred as she nuzzled my hand. Liam had the amazing ability to sense what animals were feeling, but I didn't need that special power to know what Minnie felt at that moment. She loved me unconditionally. Just like my grandparents.

I couldn't help but feel like a burden to Grams and Papa. Especially after all I'd put them through. Yet, they continued to love me through all of it. No amount of chores I could ever do would equal what they had done for me.

With one last pat on Minnie's head I went inside. For once, Grams wasn't in the kitchen. Instead, she and Papa were in the living room standing in front of the TV. Grams' hands covered her mouth while Papa's jaw worked back and forth.

I joined them, but neither one of them acknowledged me. I looked to the TV to find the same reporter from the night before on the screen.

"Fire crews are working hard to get the fires under control," the newscaster said as she cut to a live shot of what looked like a restaurant set ablaze. Firemen held large hoses directed at the flames. "It is believed that the staff and customers were evacuated safely."

"Where's that at?" I asked.

"Beloit," Papa grumbled. "That's not the only fire."

"How many more?"

"Two," Grams said. "A church and a farm house."

At that moment, an image of a little house with red and orange flames shooting out of the windows appeared on the screen. Fire trucks and police cars surrounded the home.

"Lord, please let that family be okay," Grams prayed.

Another image of what used to be a church was displayed. Half a dozen people clutched each other as they stood around a steaming pile of rubble.

The reporter returned. "Police believe these were acts of arson but have no suspects yet. We'll keep you updated as we receive new information."

It seemed all Hell had broken loose in the small town of Beloit. First the murder and rape last night, and now these fires. And it was all happening too close for comfort.

I prayed that whoever was causing this mayhem wouldn't bring it into Despair.

CHAPTER FIVE

I WOKE FROM MY DREAM IN a cold sweat. It was identical to the one I'd had the night before. Once again, I was in the long hallway full of portraits and mirrors. The boy in the painting warned me to stay away from the triangle mirror. I tried to resist, but an invisible force pulled me toward it. When Jeremy appeared through the blue fog, I tried to force myself awake before he could reveal his face, but it didn't work. It wasn't until he grabbed my throat that I jerked awake.

What did it mean? Why did I have it again?

My former therapist said that dreams were a way for our minds to manifest our subconscious fears, fantasies, and joys. She'd said that any dream could be interpreted. I had no idea where to even begin to interpret this one.

It was four in the morning, but I knew I wouldn't be able to go back to sleep. There was no use laying there and torturing myself. I got out of bed and traded my sweaty T-shirt for a clean one. As I padded to the kitchen, I synced my footsteps to the ticking of the living room clock.

In the kitchen, I grabbed a glass from the cabinet and filled it with water from the faucet. As I guzzled the liquid, I stared out the window above the sink. It was too dark to see anything except for the stable a dozen yards away which was illuminated by small lights hanging from the exterior.

My heart leapt into my throat and I spit water into the sink. I leaned against the counter and squinted. "What in the world?"

Was my mind playing tricks on me again? It looked like

somebody was standing beside the stable just beyond the lights. A shudder crept up my spine. I closed my eyes and shook my head. When I opened them, I looked to the same spot. Nobody was there.

I rubbed my hands over my face. "You need sleep, Nina Anderson."

With a leery eye still on the window, I placed my glass in the sink and tiptoed to the back door, checking the lock before leaving the kitchen.

THERE WAS NOTHING ON the local TV stations at five in the morning. I was sprawled out on the couch watching an infomercial when Papa hobbled into the living room.

"Mornin', sweet pea," he said, rubbing the sleep from his eyes.

He and Grams had stopped asking me long ago why I was up so early. Maybe one day I'd actually be able to sleep.

"Good morning," I said. "I'm surprised Grams isn't up yet."

"She was praying most of the night for the people affected by the fires. She finally conked out a couple of hours ago."

My reoccurring nightmare seemed so trivial compared to the victims of the fires. Why would somebody do such a thing? Hopefully nobody had been hurt.

With a grunt, Papa eased into his recliner. The simple act seemed to drain all of his energy.

I reached my hand out and touched his arm. "How are you feeling this morning?"

He shrugged as he stared at the TV. "No better. No worse."

"When's your next appointment?"

"In a few days."

"Will you do another round of chemo?"

Papa released a long sigh. "Unfortunately, yes."

My prayer every night was that the chemotherapy would pulverize the cancer, but I was afraid my prayers were falling on deaf ears. At times I felt prayer was pointless. God was going to do whatever He wanted. My dad had been in a vegetative state after being hit by a car, and I'd prayed unceasingly for a miracle. I never got the miracle. And at eighteen years old I had to make the gut-wrenching decision to take him off of life support.

God owed me. Cancer took my mother before I got to know her. Surely he wouldn't let it take my Papa too. If Papa did go into remission, would he be able to bounce back? What if the cancer returned? He wouldn't be strong enough to endure treatments again.

Papa looked in my direction, giving me a sweet smile. "Stop worrying."

I sat up. "How do you know I'm worrying?" He pointed to the space between his bushy eyebrows. "You see these deep lines? Those aren't smile lines, sweet pea. With all the worrying you do, you'll wind up having a permanent scowl."

I relaxed my brows and slumped my shoulders. "I can't help it."

"How are *you*? You're not working today are you?"

"I'm going to call in. I don't think I could stand being there today." Plus I'd made a promise to Liam that I wouldn't go.

"That's probably a good idea."

Papa and I watched meaningless television until it was light enough to go outside. I stood, heading to my room to change. "I'm going to take care of the horses, Papa. Can I get you anything?"

He smiled sweetly. "No, thank you."

Once in my room, I changed into jeans and a sweatshirt, then pulled on my coat and slipped into my boots. When I opened the back door, icy air blew in. It was going to be another brisk day. I jogged to the stable and grabbed hold of the handle of the heavy door.

I couldn't help but be a little paranoid after seeing that dark figure by the stable last night. Surely it was only the lights from the barn causing a shadow. Perhaps someday I wouldn't feel the need to constantly question everything.

"Nina," a deep voice said behind me.

A scream bubbled up in my throat and I spun around. My scream halted as I stared at the face of the man who'd said my name.

Liam stood before me.

CHAPTER SIX

MY HEART SKIPPED A BEAT. WHY was he here? Better yet, how was he here? Wait, that didn't matter. He was right in front of me. The best question was, why wasn't I already in his arms?

I smiled as I threw myself at Liam, wrapping my arms around his neck and locking my legs around his waist. A normal man would have stumbled with the force of our colliding bodies. But Liam was far from normal. He didn't sway an inch.

I leaned back so I could look him in the eye. "What does this mean? Are you free of the conditions?"

Liam frowned, shaking his head. His eyes didn't hold their usual sparkle. I unwound my legs and planted my feet on the ground.

Liam pulled my hands from around his neck. "We need to talk."

My brow wrinkled. Bad news always followed the words, "we need to talk." I took a deep breath, trying to gear myself up for whatever it was he was about to tell me.

Liam pulled open the stable door and led me to a hay bale. I took a seat, curling my legs beneath me and tucking my cold hands between my knees. Liam remained in front of me, walking back and forth as he squeezed the nape of his neck. It wasn't often that Liam was anxious. I was usually the one to fret about something.

"Just tell me what's going on, Liam."

He stopped pacing and looked at me, taking in a shaky breath. I'd never seen him so rattled. I wanted nothing more than to take away whatever was causing him so much grief.

Liam knelt in front of me so that we were eye to eye. He opened his mouth to speak, but then shook his head. "I don't even know where to begin."

"First, tell me if being outside the clearing is permanent."

His frown deepened. "No."

My chest tightened. I think I had already known the answer, but I needed to hear it from him. "Does this have something to do with why you left last night?"

"Yes."

My stomach somersaulted. "What is it?"

"I left to report your story about Carl to..." He paused as he tried to find the right words.

"You can't tell me who, can you?"

He sighed. "Let's call them the Martyr High Council."

"Is this high council a bunch of old guys in white robes sitting on thrones? Because that's what I'm picturing right now."

Liam smiled. "Creative, but no."

I snapped my fingers. "Darn." I shoved my hair behind my ears. "Okay, then, what did the high council say?"

Liam released a long sigh. "Carl is being controlled by a Rogue."

My heart sank. I'd dismissed the idea last night, but it was true? I narrowed my eyes. "How do you know?"

"His behavior, his eyes, his scent, they're all clear signs." Liam placed a hand on my knee. His body stiffened and his eyes seemed to beg me to really hear him. "I know this is hard to believe, but it's true. You need to know about the Rogues since you've come face to face with one."

I didn't want to be privy to any of this information. I wanted a simple life. I wanted to wake up from a good night's sleep, go to a job where I could earn enough money for a comfortable living, go home to a loving husband, and do it all over again the next day. But I had to come to terms with the fact that as long as I loved

Liam, I was never going to have a normal life.

The world I thought I knew had already been turned upside down a few months before when I discovered there were Angel-like beings with superpowers being sent to Earth to protect humans. How much weirder could things get?

I crossed my arms. "Okay. Lay it on me."

LIAM COULDN'T HELP BUT smile at Nina's determination. It seemed no matter what he told her, she would absorb the initial shock, then figure out the best way to handle the information. It was because of him that Nina was so wrapped up in his immortal world in the first place. If he couldn't tell her what she wanted to know about Martyrs, he could at least tell her everything he knew about Rogues.

He relaxed slightly and cleared his throat before beginning. "A Rogue is dormant in the host that it inhabits until it's ready to use the host's body. The smell of vinegar is an indicator that a Rogue is present within a human. And you said Carl's eyes dilated right before he pulled the gun, correct?" Nina nodded.

"And did his personality seem to change?"

"Yes. He became agitated all of a sudden."

"The Rogue chose that moment to act. Carl didn't have any control over his actions."

Nina held up her hands. "Hold on a minute. Let's start at the beginning. Where do Rogues even come from?"

Liam moved to sit beside Nina on the hay bale. She shifted so she could face him.

"It's called The Inbetween. It's the realm between Earth and Hell."

Nina's brows rose. "What do Rogues look like?"

"They don't have a corporeal form. I've never seen one, but it's said that outside of a host, they resemble mist."

Nina's eyes widened. Her gaze shifted and she lifted her thumb to her lips, nibbling on the nail.

It was so hard for Liam to not listen to her thoughts at that moment. Truth was, he loved to hear what she was thinking. She had a brilliant mind. And that mind was so connected to her heart. She didn't choose one over the other, she made all her decisions based on both, even if they contradicted each other. She was rational, yet passionate. Stubborn, yet sensitive.

Even though Liam had the ability to know what Nina was thinking, there was still so much to discover about her. Every day, he learned something new. And each day, he fell a little more in love with her.

Nina met Liam's gaze once again. "How do Rogues find a host?"

"All humans have free will to choose good or evil. And all humans choose evil at one time or another. Rogues seek out the humans who are choosing evil more and more often. Those who used to steal a penny and have come to the place where stealing a dollar is of no consequence. The Rogues encourage those people to take the final plunge."

Nina closed her eyes and rubbed at her forehead. "How do they know if somebody is leaning toward evil?" Her eyes sprang open. "And how do they get inside that person's body?"

"While Martyrs only hear the thoughts of their assignments, Rogues can hear what anybody is thinking. If they hear something that indicates a human is toeing the line between good and evil, then they've found their perfect victim. We don't know how they enter the body. Nobody in Martyr history has seen it happen."

Nina wrapped her arms around her middle. "Is there any way to get a Rogue out?"

"Not without destroying the body they inhabit."

Nina bit her lip, and she looked away.

Liam reached for her hand. "What is it?"

Her gaze fell back to him. "Are all people who commit crimes under the influence of a Rogue?" She swallowed hard. "Was Jeremy?"

He knew she was going to ask that. She wasn't going to want to hear the answer.

"No, not all people. Some don't need a Rogue to push them over the edge." Liam's teeth gritted as he thought of the man who had harmed Nina for so long. "Jeremy was not controlled by a Rogue. Everything that he did was of his own choosing."

Nina mashed her lips together as tears filled her eyes. Liam didn't have to listen to her thoughts to know what she was thinking. She wanted everything that Jeremy did to have been out of his control. This only confirmed that he hurt her because he wanted to.

Nina closed her eyes and tears leaked out. She wiped at them before they could travel down her cheeks. Liam's heart ached every time she cried. If only he could take on her emotional pain. She'd been hurting for far too long.

Liam's brows pulled together as a thought dawned on him. Was he only adding to the hurt? Nina deserved a chance at a normal relationship. He would never be able to give her that.

Nina cleared her throat. "How do Rogues get to Earth from The Inbetween?"

"There are passages all around your world, but a human finding one is nearly impossible. It's hard enough for a Martyr."

"Are you saying there's a passage around here? Possibly in Despair?"

"We're not sure. I was temporarily released to look into it. Rogues tend to do their bidding in spurts. Have there been any recent outbreaks of crime in Despair or surrounding cities?"

Nina's eyes widened. "Yes, actually. In Beloit."

Liam's heart leapt.

"A couple of nights ago there was a murder-suicide and a

rape. Then only last night somebody set multiple fires."

Liam bent his head and rubbed at his eyes. "Just as we feared."

"So what do we do?"

Liam's head shot up. "We?"

"Well, yeah. Of course I'm going to help."

His eyes widened. "You can't, Nina. It's way too dangerous."

"Then why would you even tell me all of this?"

"You needed to know why I was here and what exactly happened with Carl. I wasn't trying to recruit you for my task to find the Rogue passage."

Nina straightened and her voice rose. "But I could be a lot of help. I know the area. And I have a car ... sort of."

Liam grabbed both of Nina's hands. "I can't put you at risk." He swallowed over the tightness in his throat. "I almost lost you once. I can't do it again."

Nina released a sigh and leaned forward, resting her forehead against his.

Liam knew he hadn't convinced her. She wasn't going to give up that easily. She was the type of woman who wanted to fix things. If there was a problem, she needed to find a solution. But this was something much bigger than her. So big that Liam would need the backing of his peers.

CHAPTER SEVEN

LIAM WOULDN'T BE ABLE TO KEEP me from trying to help, and he wouldn't forbid me to, either. He knew how important my independence was since I'd been Jeremy's puppet for so long. Jeremy had been the ultimate puppet master. No matter how reluctant I was, he'd simply tug on a string and I'd go wherever he wanted. A pull on another string and I'd say what he desired. I would never allow anybody to control me again. I'd gnaw the strings off if I had to.

Liam was merely asking me to not get involved so that I wouldn't get hurt. I understood that, and I didn't want him to worry about me, but I could be useful in finding the Rogue passage. I'd ridden Hezzie for miles past the farm and driven through the rolling hills so much that I felt I'd been the maker of the land. Even if the passage wasn't around Despair, I could help Liam get to the surrounding areas.

He'd said Rogues didn't have a physical form, but rather resemble a type of mist. I couldn't help but think back to the fog that had swirled behind the mirror within my dream. However, the dream was only that. It wasn't reality. But if I truly felt that it didn't mean anything, then why was I continuing to hide it from Liam? Could the current events and my dream be related somehow? Internally, I shook it off and rejected the idea.

Liam pulled his forehead away from mine and squinted at me. He was trying so hard not to listen to my thoughts, but he wanted to. I smiled and pressed my lips to his, hopefully distracting him from the temptation to read my mind.

Liam cupped my cheeks and deepened the kiss. Heat pooled in my belly, and I felt tingles all the way to my toes. If he was trying to erase my thoughts completely, then it was working. Liam removed his lips from mine sooner than I was ready for. I kept my eyes closed as I waited for the residual effects of this type of kiss. Goosebumps sprouted across my arms, and for a moment I forgot how to breathe.

I opened my eyes to look into Liam's. Was that heat in his eyes? Did Martyrs feel . . . that?

"Yes, Nina, I do," he said in a husky tone. "I may not be human, but I still have all the normal feelings and desires of a man."

I felt blood rush to my cheeks as I ignored the fact that he'd listened to my candid thought. I glanced at his lips and licked my own. The electric pull of attraction between us was too much to take. I cleared my throat and stood, striding over to Hezzie.

We needed to change the subject—get back to the task at hand. I stroked Hezzie's nose. "So, James Bond, why did the Martyr High Council choose you to carry out this mission?"

Liam joined me at Hezzie's pen, leaning against the gate. "Who's James Bond?"

I waved my hand. "Doesn't matter. Are they making you do this?"

He shook his head. "They're not making me do anything. I volunteered."

"Why?"

"For two reasons. One, I don't want any more people to get hurt."

"And the other?"

His mouth shifted to the side, and he averted his gaze. "It's selfish really."

"Why?"

His eyes met mine once again. "I knew I'd be free of the clearing. Therefore, I could be with you more than two hours a day."

With a smile, I grabbed Liam's hand. "Well, then I'm glad you were selfish."

The impassioned look he gave me made my stomach somersault. I pulled my hand away slowly and shoved my hands in my coat pockets. "So, how will you find the passage?"

Liam shrugged a muscular shoulder. "I need to track down other Martyrs in the area."

"How will you do that? Send out some kind of bat signal?"

"A what?"

"A special signal like Batman does."

Liam's brows wrinkled. "Who is Batman?"

"He's a . . . forget it. Someday maybe we can watch all these movies I make references to that you don't understand."

My heart dropped at the realization that we would never have a chance to do that. We'd never be a normal couple who goes on dates, or does something as simple as watch movies.

I gave my head a quick shake before I thought about it so much that I became depressed. "Will you take the Martyrs away from their assignments?"

Liam rubbed at the stubble on his chin. "I'll ask them to assist me so long as it doesn't interfere with their first priority. I know that the Martyrs who visit their former assignments in Despair will be happy to serve the cause."

"Like Lulu's Martyr, Kimmie?"

Liam's head titled to the side. "How do you know about Kimmie?"

"That night I babysat Lulu she told me she had a Martyr when she was two. She said Kimmie still visits her." A murderous ex-boyfriend had prevented me from finding out how that was possible. If I would have gotten the answer, I wouldn't have been so distraught for the three months that I thought Liam was dead.

"Where does Kimmie go to visit Lulu anyway? And does she have the two-hour regulation as well?"

"Yes, she does. I'm not sure where she goes to see Lulu. Martyrs who revisit their assignments usually meet in a place that is special to them."

"Like our clearing."

Liam smiled. "Exactly."

It would have been a lot more convenient to meet Liam in the barn. However, the clearing had always been our place. And forever would be.

"So do you think Kimmie will help?"

Liam nodded slowly.

My brows shot up. "Can I meet her?"

"If you'd like."

I was finally going to meet another Martyr. What would she look like? When I'd first met Liam, he said Martyrs appeared in a way that caught their assignment's attention. What would get Lulu's attention? But that wasn't the important matter. I needed to find out all I could about this Rogue situation so that I could find a way to help.

I cleared my throat. "What will you do once you find the passage?"

"Destroy it."

"How?"

"Each passage has a leader. If we take out the leader, then the passage and everything within it or that has ever passed through it ceases to exist."

"Will the people inhabited by a Rogue die as well?"

"Unfortunately, yes."

That didn't seem fair. Even though those taken over by a Rogue had already chosen to follow their wicked inclinations, didn't they deserve a chance for redemption? If a Rogue exited their body maybe they would then choose good over evil. Hopefully, we'd be able to find the passage before more Rogues passed through and found their hosts. Even immoral people were worth saving.

"How will you take out the leader?" I asked.

Liam grabbed a sugar cube from a bucket near his feet. He tossed the cube back and forth between his hands. "It won't be easy. That's why I need more help. Rogue leaders have supernatural powers that can even affect Martyrs."

My brows rose. "Seriously? That's not very encouraging."

"It takes a lot for the powers to work on us, but it's possible."

"What exactly can the leader do?"

Liam filled up his cheeks with air and let it out slowly. "For one, they can cause temporary paralysis."

A shiver crept up my spine. "How long does it last?"

Liam held out the sugar cube he'd been holding to Hazel. She snatched it out of his palm with her lips. "I don't know. Hopefully I'll never have to find out."

"What else?"

"They create hallucinations. Because of their ability to hear thoughts, they know a person's greatest fears and desires and can use that against them."

I swallowed hard.

"Their greatest power is that of persuasion. They can convince you to think, do, or say anything, making it seem like it was all your idea."

Maybe it would be harder to help than I'd thought. Still, I couldn't let Liam go at this alone. We were a team. And I wasn't near as breakable as he thought me to be. I loved that he always wanted to protect me, but I couldn't sit back and allow him to fight this battle on his own. No matter what came our way, I would be by his side. Just as I knew he would be by mine.

Liam stepped closer, gazing down at me. "Now do you understand how dangerous this all is?" He pushed a strand of hair behind my ear. "You're incredibly strong, but also very fragile. If I lost you…" He bit down on his lip and looked away.

When his eyes landed back on me, they were filled with determination. He grabbed my hands. They felt so tiny enveloped in his. "I can't let anything happen to you again."

Butterflies danced in my stomach. I loved this man so much. I went to my tiptoes, pressing my lips to his. Liam wrapped his arms around my back, tugging me against him. The passion between us was too much to handle. I told myself I was going to end the kiss any second.

Just as I was about to lose myself completely, a throat cleared. Liam and I jerked away from each other to stare in the direction of the barn entrance.

Papa stood in the doorway, his lips pressed firmly together.

CHAPTER EIGHT

SHOCK AND CONFUSION PASSED OVER PAPA'S face. His gaze flicked from Liam, to me, and back again.

I took a step toward him. "Papa . . ." I swallowed hard. Where did I even begin? "I know this is crazy."

With a quizzical brow, he shuffled to Liam, stopping directly in front of him. He stared up at him without a word. What was he thinking?

Liam looked at me briefly, before turning his attention to Papa. The slightest twitch in Liam's left eye told me he was worried about my grandfather's reaction.

The crease in Papa's forehead smoothed, and he stuck out his palm. Liam reached out, clasping Papa's hand. The two stared at each other as they shook hands.

"I don't know what you are, but you brought my Nina back to life. For that, I am eternally grateful," Papa said firmly.

A lump lodged in my throat and tears filled my eyes.

Liam nodded and gave Papa a light smile. The two released their grips, and Papa turned to me.

"Papa, I . . ." A tear rolled down my cheek.

He came to me and tugged on my left ear lobe. "I don't need an explanation, sweet pea. I understand why you didn't want to tell me."

I wiped at the tear clinging to my chin. "I'm sorry I kept it a secret. I wanted to tell you so many times."

Papa placed his hands on my shoulders. "It's okay. Your secret is safe with me."

He pulled me toward him, draping his arms around my back in a tight hug. I wrapped my own arms around his waist. Relief washed over me. All this time I'd been so afraid to tell him. I should have known he'd be supportive. I could have saved myself a lot of anguish if I'd taken a leap of faith and trusted him.

Papa broke the hug and wiped the moisture from my cheeks. "At least now I know you're safe when you go on your nightly rides."

I breathed out a laugh. "Probably the safest place on the planet."

I looked to Liam, and he shot me a wink. My cheeks flushed.

Papa mockingly glared at Liam. "Don't think for one second that just because you're a powerful . . . well, whatever you are, that I won't try to take you down if you do something to hurt my Nina."

Liam smiled. "Of course not, sir. But you don't have to worry." He looked to me again. His gaze made my heartrate quicken. "I love her with all that I am and will never hurt her."

My heart soared. For a moment, I forgot that Papa was in the barn with us. It wasn't until he cleared his throat that I shook my head and turned my attention back to him.

Papa gave us a quick wave. "You two kids have a good afternoon. I'm headed into town."

My chest seized. I didn't want him going anywhere. Who knew what could happen to him with Rogues roaming around. "What do you need in town? Liam and I could get it for you."

"Nah, that's alright. I'd like to get off the farm for a bit anyway." He turned around and headed for the exit.

I couldn't let him go. He was too weak to be able to defend himself if somebody, or rather something, attacked him. I took a step in his direction. "Papa, please don't go."

He spun back around, his brow wrinkling. "What's going on, sweet pea?"

My gaze shot to Liam. *How much can I tell him?*

49

Liam nodded once.

I swallowed hard and looked to Papa. "There's something happening that I can't quite explain, but you need to be very careful."

His brows furrowed further. "Does this have to do with the fires and the craziness in Beloit?"

I nodded slowly. "And Carl."

Papa's eyes widened. "What is it?"

"Carl isn't himself right now." I shook my head. "I can't give you more details than that. Please don't leave the farm unless absolutely necessary, Papa. And if you have to leave, then watch your back."

Papa pointed at me. "What about you? You're the one who's always roaming around the farm."

"I have this guy." I nudged Liam in the shoulder. "And I'm tougher than you both think."

Papa released a sigh as he scrubbed his hand over his bald head. Rough palms chafed across his speckled skin. His eyes landed on Liam. "Is whatever is going on the reason you're here?"

Liam cleared his throat. "Yes, sir."

"Anything I can do to help?"

"Just be on the lookout for anything suspicious. And keep yourself safe."

Papa crossed his arms. "Nina isn't getting involved in this is she?"

"No."

"Not yet, anyway," I added, shooting Liam a look.

"Not ever," he said firmly.

"She's a stubborn one," Papa said. "She'll find a way to try to help."

One corner of Liam's mouth lifted. "I'm well aware."

I rolled my eyes. "Could you two stop talking about me like I'm not standing right here?"

Papa chuckled. "We love you for your stubbornness, sweet

pea. Wouldn't have it any other way."

I planted my hands on my hips. "I inherited it from you and Grams."

"Yep. You were doomed." Papa shot us another quick wave and left the barn.

My shoulders slumped and I released a loud sigh. Papa was exactly like me. He liked to fix things. He'd be cautious, but he wasn't going to leave this alone. I could only hope and pray that he was too drained to try to get involved.

CHAPTER NINE

I DIDN'T WANT TO GO BACK to work. Not because I was afraid, but because I wanted to spend all of my time with Liam. But I still had responsibilities that I couldn't shirk because the love of my life was on a temporary hiatus from his confinement.

It had been two days since Liam was freed, and he'd taken up residence in the barn. It felt a little like old times. The circumstances were slightly different. And hopefully the ending wouldn't be the same.

"I still don't feel good about this," Liam said from the passenger seat of Old Blue.

I pulled into the parking lot behind the bank and stopped the truck. "I have to go back sometime. I need the money." I lifted the parking brake and turned to him. "Besides, this is the perfect opportunity for you to track down more Martyrs."

He reached over, stroking my cheek. "I won't be far should you need me."

I leaned into his touch, giving his wrist a quick kiss. "I'll be fine. Now go scrounge up the other Avengers to save the world."

The corner of his mouth curved. "Is that another movie reference?"

I smiled. "Hey, you're catching on." I unbuckled and slid out of the truck. When I turned to shut the door, Liam was no longer in his seat.

"I want to make sure you get inside safely," he said at my ear.

His unexpected appearances at my side used to startle me.

Not anymore. I more than welcomed them. I came to my toes and planted a kiss on his lips before heading for the back entrance to the bank. When I reached the door, I glanced behind me to find Liam leaning against the bumper. Even though I didn't share his talent for mind-reading, I was getting better at reading his body language and noticing the slightest change in his expression.

His squared shoulders told me he'd protect me no matter what. The slight wrinkle in his brow indicated he was worried about leaving me. He'd lay down his life for me time and time again. As would I. But he would never allow it.

Why did he believe my life had more value than his? Because he wasn't human? I'd lost him once. I couldn't allow it to happen another time. Whatever was to come with the Rogues, I'd do anything I could to keep him from dying in my arms again. Even though Martyrs' spirits couldn't truly die, and I was sure Liam would come back to me should something happen, I couldn't stand watching his physical form suffer.

I blew Liam a quick kiss and stepped into the building. As I came around the corridor to the entrance of the lobby, a muscled arm reached out to stop me. My eyes widened and I jumped back. The stern face of a stocky policeman stared down at me.

"You work here?" the man asked without a hint of a smile.

My boss, Mr. Wright, jogged out of his office. "She's one of my tellers," he said, pushing his glasses up the bridge of his long nose.

The policeman's expression didn't change as he dropped his arm. I nodded to the man and made my way to the front of the building. Mr. Wright followed me.

"What's with the extra muscle?" I asked.

"It's a precaution. Just in case."

"Carl would be pretty stupid to come back." However, it wasn't really Carl who had done it in the first place. Would the Rogue come back? Could I be in danger being here?

"Nina!" Kaley said when I reached the lobby. She ran to me,

wrapping her arms around my shoulders. She released the hug and looked me right in the eyes. "Why weren't you here yesterday?"

"I needed a day off to recoup. Did you work?"

She nodded.

Hadn't she been scared running the desk by herself? I should have been here for her. I would have hated working alone. Well, she wasn't completely alone if the police officer had been here. But based on our initial encounter, he didn't seem very warm and fuzzy. Hopefully Mr. Wright had lent a listening ear.

Mr. Wright pulled at his belt loops, hiking up his pants. "I'll be in my office if you ladies need anything. And Officer Hays is here all day." He pointed to the big man I'd run into. He now stood at the front entrance with a stoic expression. Would he be able to protect us if we needed it?

Mr. Wright strode into his office, and I plopped down on my stool. Kaley did the same. "You doing okay?" I asked.

Her shoulders rose and fell. "I haven't been able to sleep. I keep seeing that crazy look in Carl's eyes. It was like he was possessed."

She had no idea how right she was.

LIAM WISHED THERE WAS a special trick to finding other Martyrs, such as a call he could cry out to have them come running. Thankfully, the elders had given him the names of the Martyrs currently visiting former assignments or residing in Despair as they carried out their tasks. Now all he had to do was find them.

Nina would be shocked to know how many Martyrs were on Earth at one time. She had more than likely passed a dozen a day while living in New York. But she would have perceived them as another nameless face in a big city.

In a small town like Despair, people would notice a stranger roaming through their city. And with everything that had happened recently, paranoia was high. Therefore, Liam had to be careful to not be seen.

I PUFFED UP MY cheeks and blew the air out slowly. Had only one hour passed? With zero customers? Maybe people were afraid to come to the bank. I couldn't blame them. Carl's robbery was the second most traumatic event to ever happen to this town. Jeremy's attack was the first.

An involuntary shiver shook my body. I'd had that same dream last night. I'd forced myself awake when Jeremy's hand clasped around my throat, but maybe I needed to let it play out. To see what happened next. But what if killing me was what happened next? And why in the world was I continuing to have the dream? I still hadn't told Liam that the hooded man was Jeremy. I didn't know why. Perhaps I feared his judgment. Though I should have realized by now that Liam was the least judgmental being.

With a yawn, I stretched my arms above my head and turned to Kaley. "Was it this slow yesterday?"

She nodded. "I think Carl scared them off." She tapped her fingers on her knees. "You know what I can't figure out? Why didn't he shoot us?"

I continued to ask myself that same question. Could it have been because deep down Carl didn't want to hurt us and had kept the Rogue from pulling the trigger?

I lifted one shoulder. "I'm not sure."

Kaley nibbled at her fingernails. "He had to have known we would report him. Do you think he wanted to be caught?"

"I don't know what was going through his mind, Kaley." I

smiled gently. "I'm only thankful that we're both okay."

The fluorescent lights above us suddenly buzzed and flickered. The computer screens flicked off, followed by all the lights. My chest tightened.

"Has this happened before?" Officer Hays asked.

Kaley jumped down from her stool. "A few times since I've been here."

Mr. Wright came out of his office, becoming merely a shadow in the hallway. "It's an old building with wiring problems. I need to flip the breaker."

"Where's the breaker box?" I asked.

Mr. Wright hooked his thumb behind him. "In the utility room near the back door."

"I'll escort you, Mr. Wright," the policeman said.

He shook his head. "That's not necessary."

"It's my job, sir."

Mr. Wright shrugged and spun on his heel, heading down the hallway with Officer Hays in tow.

Even though sun poured in through the front windows, the lobby felt eerily dim. I resisted the urge to bite at my fingernails. "This seems pretty coincidental; don't you think?"

Kaley's brows furrowed. "What do you mean?"

I shook my head. "Never mind." No need to spook her as well.

A breaker blew, Nina. There's no need to be scared. But after everything that had occurred within the last year, I had every right to be a tad suspicious.

"Kaley, could you bring a flashlight?" Mr. Wright's voice called from the hallway.

Kaley pulled open a drawer and dug around before pulling out a Maglite. "I'll be back," she said, flipping it on and heading down the corridor.

I was alone. And the lobby was far too quiet. I tapped my fingers on the counter and glanced down the hallway. A shiver crept up my spine. How long did it take to flip a switch? My teeth caught my bottom lip. This was silly. I didn't need to be afraid.

"Do you guys need help?" I called.

No response.

I hopped off my stool and strode toward the shadowy hallway. I didn't know how I'd be able to help. I knew next to nothing about anything electrical. As I made my way down the hallway, it seemed to grow darker. And was it getting longer and narrower? I stopped, placing my hand on the wall to get my bearings. A wave of wooziness struck me. I shouldn't have skipped breakfast.

The room swayed and I took a deep breath, allowing the dizzy spell to dissipate. When it did, I set off again, but my feet wouldn't move. I glanced down, expecting my shoes to be caught on something. Nothing but the floor spread out before me.

My heart rate quickened. What in the world? *Move feet!* But they wouldn't obey. It was as though my brain couldn't relay the message.

This is a dream. I'm going to wake up any second, and I'll be cozy in my bed.

"Help!" I screamed as I jerked my waist from side to side, trying to get my feet to move. They remained immobile.

The lights suddenly blinked on. My feet jerked and propelled me forward. I stumbled, crashing to the floor.

"Nina?" Mr. Wright called. He, Kaley, and the officer came around the corner toward me.

My heart raced. With wide eyes, I glanced up and down the hallway.

Kaley gripped my shoulders, pulling me to stand. "What happened?"

"Nina, what's wrong?" *Liam.* He was suddenly by my side, pulling me away from Kaley.

"Who are you?" Officer Hays asked.

Liam ignored him as he swiped my hair from my forehead.

He held my face in his hands, staring into my eyes with a frantic look that I was sure I shared. "What happened?"

"I . . . I couldn't move."

Liam pulled his head back and his brows wrinkled. With a sigh, he ran his hand over his face. "Let's get you out of here." He grabbed my hand, hauling me toward the back entrance.

"Wait, who are you?" Mr. Wright asked. "Nina, do you want to go with this man?"

I closed my eyes briefly, trying to get hold of the panic coursing through my body. My racing heart slowed slightly, and I opened my eyes. "Yes. I'm fine. Please, don't worry about me." Before I could explain more, Liam led us through the back door.

CHAPTER TEN

LIAM HELPED ME INTO THE PASSENGER seat of Old Blue and was in the driver's seat himself in less than a second. He didn't force me to speak as he drove us home. Occasionally, he would lightly touch my knee, or rub at the nape of my neck. Those small touches kept me grounded. Kept me from screaming. Just when I thought I was calm, the panic would seize my chest again, and I'd have to start the whole process over of reassuring myself that I was safe.

Liam stopped the truck in front of my grandparents' mailbox, leaving the truck idling. He leaned back in his seat. I felt him looking at me as I stared unseeingly at the dash in front of me.

"What happened to me back there, Liam?"

"The Rogue leader happened."

I jerked my head in his direction. "He was there?"

Liam nodded slowly. "It's the only explanation for why you couldn't move." His body remained calm, but I could see in his eyes that he was trying not to panic. He was keeping it together for my sake. "Have you been having anymore strange dreams?"

I sucked in a shaky breath and let it out slowly through pursed lips. "Not new ones. The last few nights I've had the same one I told you about."

"Is there anything different about it?"

I swallowed hard and knotted my fingers together. "The man in black has Jeremy's face."

Liam chewed on his lower lip, his brows pulling together as he gazed out the windshield.

"What are you thinking?" I whispered.

"I'm trying to figure something out."

"What?"

"Why the Rogue leader is attacking you. The only thing I can think of is that he's using you to get to me. Playing on your fear of Jeremy to mess with your dreams wasn't enough." Liam squeezed his eyes shut and pinched the bridge of his nose. "Now he's coming after you in the flesh."

I swallowed hard and ignored my racing heart. "How could the leader know about Jeremy or even the fact that I'm connected to you?"

Liam's eyes sprang open. "Rogues can read your thoughts, remember?" He rubbed at the nape of his neck. "We're going to get to the bottom of this." He turned to me and grabbed my hand. "I promise I won't let anything happen to you."

I gave him a small smile. The tension in my shoulders and the tightness in my chest eased as Liam used his peculiar power to calm my nerves. I knew he wouldn't let anything happen to me, as I wouldn't let anything happen to him.

"Were you able to find any other Martyrs while you were in town?"

"I did indeed. Three. Kimmie was one of them."

My brows shot up. "Are they all going to help?"

"They are."

Exhilaration shot through my veins. I gripped Liam's arm. "That's great." Perhaps we could beat the Rogues after all.

He smiled slightly.

"You don't seem very thrilled about it."

"The four of us won't be enough."

Liam was the strongest being I knew. With four Martyrs together, they could easily take on a human army. But perhaps a Rogue army was much stronger. "How many Martyrs do you need?"

"More than four, I know that much."

"Where are the three of them now?"

"They should be waiting for me at the clearing."

I sat forward, every nerve alert. "Can I come with you?" The thought of meeting other Martyrs made me giddy.

His thumb grazed back and forth across my knuckles. "Nina, I told you I don't want you to get involved with this. Especially after what just happened."

"Please? I just want to meet them."

Liam shifted his mouth to the side.

"I'll say hi, and then I'll leave you to take care of your business. I promise."

He released a defeated growl. "You're really hard to say no to. You know that?"

A smile spread across my face. "Is that a yes then?"

"It's a yes."

I squeezed his arm. Finally, I was going to meet other Martyrs.

Liam sighed. "I want you with me anyway."

I searched the dark pools of his eyes. They held such love and concern for me. I didn't deserve this man. Being with Jeremy had taught me that. I pushed the thought away before Liam heard it. He'd taught me so much about what real love was—nothing at all like the selfish, even cruel counterfeit Jeremy had offered.

Liam tucked a strand of hair behind my ear. "As if I wasn't worried about you enough already."

I tapped his nose. "You need to stop worrying about me and focus on finding that passage so that this can all go away."

My stomach sank. But then Liam would once again be confined to the clearing, and we'd have to go back to our daily visits that weren't nearly long enough. The whole situation was a double-edged sword.

He smiled. "I'll never stop worrying about you. I love you."

"Not as much as I love you."

"Doubtful."

He leaned forward and soft lips caressed mine. Nothing mattered in that moment except us.

I pulled away first, my cheeks flushing. "You're going to keep your friends waiting."

"They'll live." His lips found mine once again. Soon the heater of the truck was no longer needed.

Liam's lips abandoned mine before I was ready. "We should go," he said.

I kept myself from pouting as I resettled into the passenger seat.

Liam opened the driver's side door. A cool breeze wafted in, making me shudder. "You go park. I'll wait here," he said.

"I think we should leave the truck here. I don't want my grandparents to know I'm home. They'll only bombard me with questions about why I'm not at work."

"Good point." Liam turned off the engine and tossed me the keys. I shoved them into my coat pocket.

"Shall we?" he asked.

I zipped my jacket up to my chin. "Yep. Let's go."

We both hopped out, meeting at the front of the truck. Liam smiled down at me as he grabbed my hand. We set out on our small trek across the grassy field I'd become so accustomed to. I'd traveled it on Hezzie so many times there was a trampled path. We headed toward it, and long, tan weeds flicked at my calves, snagging on my dress pants. Too bad I didn't have a change of clothes in the truck.

Liam was silent on the way. His eyes darted from side to side, scanning the surrounding trees and fields. He had every right to be paranoid. I, however, wasn't concerned at all. With Liam by my side, I had nothing to fear.

But as we neared our infamous row of trees, my anxiety began to rise. What would the other Martyrs be like? Would they be as sweet and caring as Liam? Dozens of questions flooded my mind, and by the time we reached the trees, I'd chewed off the

ends of my nails on the hand Liam wasn't holding.
Liam turned to me before we walked through. "They're going to love you. You ready?"

I took a deep breath, holding in the clean, autumn air. "I'm ready," I said on an exhale.

Liam released my hand to shove aside the branches, clearing a path to squeeze through. I followed closely behind, ducking and twisting to avoid being impaled.

When I stepped through to the clearing, my breath caught in my throat. The flowers somehow seemed taller, brighter, more vibrant. Hundreds of fragrances vied for my attention, each one sweeter than the last. The water of the pond was as blue as an ocean, and I swear a tropical fish jumped out and did a flip.

But of all the beauty, nothing compared to the three beings standing before me.

CHAPTER ELEVEN

MY MOUTH DROPPED OPEN. THE THREE Martyrs stared at me, their expressions unreadable, but the love pouring out from them was palpable.

"Nina, I'd like for you to meet Kimmie, Damian, and Violet," Liam said. "As you know, Kimmie visits her former assignment, and Damian does as well. However, Violet is currently fulfilling her purpose."

It was obvious which one was Kimmie. Her flowing gold locks, piercing blue eyes, and pink pouty lips were stunning. She resembled a Barbie doll. I should have known. Of course Lulu's Martyr would appear to her as a life-sized Barbie.

Kimmie smiled, her eyes glinting. "Hi, Nina. It's so nice to finally meet you." Her soft voice flowed from her lips like music. "Lulu talks about you constantly."

I wanted to speak, but I couldn't find the words. She was captivating.

This is who Liam should be with. My thought was so loud and unexpected I had to look around to see if somebody else had spoken it.

I glanced at Liam. His forehead wrinkled, and he cocked his head slightly. Had he heard my thought as well? Surely he would agree with me. Kimmie was not only gorgeous, but one of his kind. Wouldn't he be happier with her?

I realized I still hadn't said anything. I shook my head lightly and cleared my throat. "It's a pleasure meeting you as well, Kimmie."

Jealousy suddenly surged through my veins. Followed by anger and irrational hatred. Wow, I hadn't felt those catty emotions since I was in high school. I took a deep breath, shoving the nasty thoughts and feelings aside. My gaze moved to the Martyr standing beside Kimmie.

Even though Martyrs didn't have an age, Damian looked to be at least eighty years old. However, his black wrinkled skin somehow looked smooth and flawless. Gray eyes peered at me from beneath bushy, white brows. A white mustache clung to his upper lip like a wispy cob web. The lifted corners of the mustache made it appear as though he were smiling, when in reality his lips remained in a straight line.

It was hard not to wonder who his assignment was. Did he appear in this way to them because he reminded them of somebody they once knew? What had he been assigned to help with?

Damian nodded in my direction. "Good morning, Miss Nina," he said with a raspy voice.

I shot him a smile before looking to the last Martyr. With alabaster skin, hair as purple as a plum, and a round baby face she couldn't have been more than fourteen. Her jade green eyes bore into mine.

"Good morning," I said.

She didn't blink, didn't smile, hardly moved.

"Violet doesn't speak," Kimmie said.

I looked to Kimmie. "She chooses not to, or she can't?"

"She was created without a voice box."

My brows drew together, and I returned my attention to Violet. "How do you communicate with your assignment?"

She continued to stare at me as if I hadn't spoken.

"Her assignment is deaf," Liam chimed in.

Well that explained it. She'd been made without a voice box because she had no use for it. I couldn't help but wonder how she was going to help us if she couldn't speak. Or, help Liam rather, not us. I kept forgetting I wasn't supposed to be involved. At least not conspicuously.

"It's so wonderful to meet you all. And I know Liam is very thankful to have your help."

Kimmie looked to Liam with a sparkle in her eye and flashed him a megawatt smile. "We're happy to help."

Liam shot her a grin back. I couldn't prevent my hands from fisting at my side. Yep, they'd be perfect together. Two gorgeous, unbreakable immortals.

Liam wrapped his arm around my waist, giving my side a gentle squeeze. Could he feel my envy?

"I'm going to take Nina back," he said to the others. "Be back soon."

Liam led us through the trees, and we walked for a time in silence. My mind couldn't help but wander to Kimmie. Sweet, beautiful, immortal Kimmie.

"You okay?" Liam asked.

"Of course. Why wouldn't I be?"

"I feel what you feel, Nina."

I blew out a quick puff of air. "You felt my jealousy then?"

"Among a multitude of other emotions. What were you jealous   of?"

I averted my gaze. "It's silly."

"Please tell me."

How could I not tell him when he asked in that honey-tinged voice of his? Besides, he could read my mind and find out if he really wanted to. Might as well tell him. I swallowed hard. "I was jealous of Kimmie."

His brows pulled together briefly. "Why?"

My shoulders rose and fell. "She's gorgeous."

"She has nothing on your beauty."

My cheeks burned. "That's not true, and you know it."

"You are the most beautiful woman I've ever seen. Inside and out."

My cheeks flushed. How was it possible for me to fall even more in love with this man? When we reached Old Blue, Liam planted a peck on my cheek. "I'll make sure you get to the house safely." He helped me into the truck and watched as I traveled up the driveway. I hopped out and waved when I got to the front porch. He returned the wave, but was gone in the time it took for me to blink.

A part of me wanted to sneak back to the clearing and eavesdrop on their conversation. Perhaps if I knew more details then I could figure out how to quietly assist. But I couldn't snoop like that. For one, I'd feel bad for being so nosy. And secondly, it wasn't safe for me to travel that far alone.

I turned for the front door. My chest tightened as I imagined Papa sitting in his chair, most likely sleeping when he'd much rather be working on the farm. Tomorrow he'd have another round of chemo. Once again, Grams and I would watch his suffering as he expelled what little substances remained in his stomach. There'd be nothing we could do to help other than bring cold compresses and water.

One of the horses suddenly screamed. I jerked my head in the direction of the barn and started to head down the stairs, but then stopped myself. My teeth clamped down on my bottom lip. No, I shouldn't go. It wasn't safe to be on my own right now.

A horse's squeal pierced the air again. What if one of them was in pain? I couldn't ignore it. I'd simply check on them quickly. What was the harm in that? I took off down the stairs and ran for the barn. The scent of hay greeted me as I slid open the door. My stomach dropped. Hezzie and Hazel were absent.

I rushed to Hezzie's pen and opened the door to the grazing field. I breathed out a sigh of relief. Both horses were strolling through the grass as though nothing were wrong. Strange. Perhaps a snake had crossed Hezzie's path. At least I wasn't on him this time.

I closed the door behind me and glanced around the stable.

A smile spread across my face. The barn was spotless. Not one speck of hay or dust covered the concrete floor. For a moment, I imagined Liam using magical powers like Cinderella to get birds and other animals to assist him.

I shoved my hands in my coat pockets and sat on Liam's hay bale pallet. A couple of rumpled blankets spread out on the bed. I picked one up and put it to my nose as I closed my eyes and inhaled deeply. Aw, honeysuckle. My favorite smell.

A horse's scream cut through the air once again. My eyes popped open and I jumped to my feet. A gasp passed my lips, and I backed against the wall.

Creepy Carl stood in front of me.

CHAPTER TWELVE

LIAM PUSHED THROUGH THE TREES AND stepped back into the clearing. The three Martyrs sat in a circle near the pond, talking about what they loved most about Earth. He watched them for a moment, observing their mannerisms and admiring their individual beauty. Though he had hoped for more help, he was thankful for what he'd been given.

Kimmie glanced at him. "Nina's just as sweet as you said she was."

Liam shot her a smile as he sat between her and Damian. "Thank you. I'm rather fond of her."

Damian absentmindedly twirled the end of his mustache. "I'm sure you're relieved to be free for a while. I know I am. Even though it's for a dangerous cause."

Liam nodded. "Any extra time I can have with Nina is worth it."

Across the circle, Violet stared at Liam, as though trying to read him. Her silence was somehow deafening.

"What is it, Violet?" he asked.

Her hands moved quickly as she signed to him. Liam considered his words carefully before answering. "I don't know what the future holds for me and Nina. It's very difficult for both of us." He released a sigh. "To answer your question, yes. I will continue meeting her here forever."

He and Nina's relationship wasn't normal, nor ideal, but it was all they had. And he cherished the moments they had together.

Violet signed again. Her question made his heart clench. "I don't know if it's what's best for her." Liam swallowed hard. "All I know is I love her."

Kimmie nudged his shoulder. "I'm very happy you've found love."

"Thank you." He tried to smile, but he couldn't seem to. Damian cleared his throat. "Shall we discuss our plan?"

Kimmie clapped her hands together. "Yes, let's talk strategy."

They all looked to Liam as though he had all the answers. He shot up a quick prayer that he wouldn't let them down.

CHAPTER THIRTEEN

I COULDN'T BREATHE. I COULDN'T MOVE. I could only stare.
Carl remained still as his dilated eyes bore into mine. His
mouth set in a straight line.

Oh, no. Oh, no.

The sound of Hezzie's hooves beating on the outer stall door
filled the silence. Out of the corner of my eye I could see Hezzie
nosing the steel bars lining the top half of the door. He wouldn't
be able to get to me.

I was on my own. I had to do something. "Carl, if you're in
there, please fight this."

The corner of Carl's mouth lifted as he released a snort. "I'm
still me, Nina. It's not as though I've been abducted by aliens and
they've taken control of my body."

But that was exactly the situation. The real Carl wouldn't be
here by his own will. Or would he? "This isn't you," I said over
the lump in my throat.

He chuckled. "Oh, but it is. I was only given the push to be
the real me."

My eyes darted around the barn, searching for a weapon. A
shovel and rake hung on the wall by the stalls. How fast was Carl?
His girth would surely slow him down. Or did the Rogue
somehow make him have super speed?

"I know what you're thinking," he said. "You're trying to
find something to defend yourself with. Or perhaps a way out. It
doesn't matter. You won't get to either in time."

Oh, God, please help me.

Carl took a step forward. I remained planted in place.

He licked his chapped lips. "I've wanted you since the day I laid eyes on you at the Farmers' Market."

My stomach coiled. This wasn't happening.

Carl took another step toward me. "It'll be quick. I promise."

With a lunge, I darted for Hezzie's pen. Carl's arms banded around me from behind before I'd reached the outside stall door.

"Help!" I screamed at the top of my lungs.

Carl's greasy hand smashed against my mouth. I pulled back my lips and sunk my teeth into his palm. He ripped it away with a snarl.

"Nobody can hear you scream anyway," he rasped at my ear. "Your grandparents are too old, and your precious Martyr is occupied at the moment."

My stomach sank.

Carl clutched my shoulders, spinning me around to face him. His eyes were black pools and as wild as a boar. "We know what he and the others are planning to do. There's no use. They can't beat us."

Carl shoved me with enough power to make me slide across the hay-strewn ground. The back of my head bounced on the cement. Spots appeared before my eyes. Hezzie squealed and stomped his hooves on the other side of the door.

Carl stepped in front of me, sweat rolling down his plump cheeks. I scrambled to my feet, only to be pushed down once more.

Liam!

Carl knelt in front of me. I scurried into the corner of the stall, huddling into myself like a cowering animal. He smiled maliciously. This was fun for him. Watching me squirm. He was a sick man. Forget what I'd originally believed that bad people were worth saving. If deep down somebody was capable of doing something like this, then the world would be a much better place without them.

His hand slowly reached toward me. My heart thumped hard in my chest, as though it were going to explode. I shoved myself further into the corner, wishing I could disappear into the wall.

Please, God, help me!

Carl was suddenly ripped away. His body flew across the barn in a blur, crashing through the gate and landing on the cement.

A second later, Liam knelt in front of me, his eyes wide with fear. "Nina, are you hurt?"

I stared at him, my mouth agape. My mind couldn't grasp the fact that he was here. He reached out to me. I jerked away from his touch. I didn't mean to. I wanted nothing more than to crawl into his lap and hold him tight.

His brows wrinkled slightly before his face became a mask of rage. He came to his feet slowly, his hands folding into fists as he stalked toward Carl who was getting to his hands and knees.

Would Liam be fast or make him suffer? Would he break his neck like he did Jeremy?

Carl grated out a laugh as he stood. He straightened slowly, looking Liam in the eye. "You won't win this. He's coming for you."

Liam made it quick. I looked away, shielding my eyes with my hands, but still able to hear the hideous snap.

I peeked through my fingers. Carl's immobile form splayed out on the ground. What happened next was something out of a sci-fi movie. A blue fog steamed from his body, becoming thicker until it wound up and away into a cyclone above his body and finally dissipated. It was there and gone within seconds.

"What was that?" I asked, breathless.

Liam's fisted hands released. "The Rogue leaving his body."

"Where does it go?"

"I don't know. But it's gone. And Carl can't hurt you now."

Liam knelt in front of me once more, his brows pulling together with concern. "Are you all right?"

I tried to hold myself together, but I couldn't. My face cracked, and the dam I was holding back let loose. Tears streamed down my face with no end in sight. I crawled to Liam, snuggling into his arms in a much-needed embrace.

LIAM HELD NINA TIGHTLY as sobs wracked her body. He'd heard her thoughts scream for help and left the other Martyrs without an explanation. If Liam had arrived at the barn a moment later, he knew what he would've walked in on. His gut clenched at the thought.

As long as Nina was involved with him, she would be in danger. The Rogues would destroy anything and anyone that got in their way of carrying out their cause. The leader must have sent Carl to hurt her. The leader wouldn't stop. He or other Rogues would continue to come after Nina. Anything to get to Liam and convince him to back down. There was only one thing to do.

Liam took a deep breath and pulled away from Nina, holding her at arms' length. He cradled her tear streaked face in his hands. Her eyes filled with anguish and fear. He didn't want to add to her pain. His heart ached knowing what he had to do. "Nina, I can't do this anymore."

Confusion passed over her face. "Do what anymore?"

He swallowed over the lump in his throat. "We can't be together."

"What are you talking about?"

"You're in too much danger being with me."

She pulled his hands from her face. "Stop. You're not doing this. I won't let you."

Tears burned Liam's eyes. He blinked them away. "Nina. We have to end this."

She bit her lip as she shook her head. "No. We don't."

She couldn't fight this. And she knew it. He didn't have to read her mind to know the moment she realized what was happening.

Her nostrils flared. "You said you'd never hurt me." Her words were like a punch to the gut. If only she knew how much it killed him to hurt her in this way. The look of betrayal on her face was far more painful than any wound he'd ever transferred to himself.

He loved her. More than she would ever know. Which was why he had to let her go—not only for her own protection but for her own happiness. He realized in that moment how selfish he'd been in keeping her. She deserved to find somebody who could love her the way he never could. She needed a mortal man.

Tears trailed down her face. She angrily wiped them away with the back of her hand.

"I'm not good for you," he said gently.

"You're the only thing good for me." Her chin trembled. "Why are you doing this?"

"Because it's what's best for you."

She touched her palm to her chest. "I choose what's best for me. You don't get to make that decision."

His heart clenched. "I already have."

Nina's face fell. Her heart was breaking, and he was the cause of it. He lightly reached behind her neck, pulling her closer so he could plant a chaste kiss on her forehead. If he didn't go now, then he never would.

Liam choked back his tears. "Goodbye, Nina."

He grabbed Carl's body and disappeared to the sound of her sobs.

CHAPTER FOURTEEN

I STARED AT THE EMPTY SPACE that Liam had occupied seconds before. Numbness filled my body and pain gripped my chest as my lungs ached for oxygen. How long had I been holding my breath? I sucked in air, the pain fading from my lungs and moving to my heart. How many times could a heart break before it stopped working altogether?

I tried to stand, but my legs were too wobbly to put weight on them. I sank back down into the hay. He'd left me. He'd actually left me. How could he do this?

I glanced at the spot on the floor where Carl had been. My hands shook as my mind replayed what had happened. What if Liam hadn't come? Would Carl have killed me after he . . . bile rose up in my throat. I leaned over, retching the contents of my stomach onto the ground.

Dragging deep breaths through my nose, I found the strength to finally stand. My knees nearly buckled. I leaned against the wall of the pen and closed my eyes. Would I ever see Liam again? The thought made another sob escape my lips. I dropped my face into my hands and slid down the wall to the floor.

Night fell as quickly as my tears. As I wallowed in my grief, my mind ran back through all the events that led to Liam ending our relationship. Did I do something wrong? Could I have done something differently? No. I didn't do anything. Which meant Liam truly did leave me to keep me safe. I wanted to be mad at him, but how could I when he was only trying to protect me?

A horse's nicker pulled me away from my self-pity. I glanced up to find Hezzie's nose pressed against the steel bars. *Oh, Hezzie.* I wiped at my tears and took a deep breath, coming to my unsteady legs. Crying wasn't going to help this situation. Liam breaking up with me wouldn't keep me from trying to help. Despair had become my town. It held two of the people I loved most in the world along with others I'd grown to care for. I couldn't sit idly by and wait for Liam and the others to defeat the Rogues.

I pulled open the stall door, allowing Hezzie into the barn. He dipped his head, waiting for me to pet him. I stroked his large jaw, staring into his glassy eyes. "Thanks for trying to help me, buddy." Tears threatened to overtake me once again.

Riding was the only other thing besides Liam that calmed me. I knew it wasn't safe, but if I didn't do something, then I'd drown in my tears. Besides, it would give me a chance to search for the passage.

First, I needed to get inside to change and check in with my grandparents. I wiped at my tear-stained face and pulled pieces of hay from my hair. Streaks of dust covered my black pants. My hands shook as I patted it off.

With a deep breath, I left the barn and headed for the house. *Please don't let my grandparents be suspicious.* I pasted on a fake smile before going in through the kitchen.

Grams stopped cutting vegetables long enough to look at me and smile. So far so good. "How did it go today?" she asked.

I swallowed over the lump in my throat. "Not bad. We were super slow." I sighed loudly. "I could really use a ride. I'm going to get changed."

I left the kitchen before Grams could interrogate me. On the way to my room, I glanced at Papa fast asleep in his recliner. I swapped my work clothes for jeans and a sweatshirt, and then pulled on my boots.

As I walked back through the kitchen I threw on my coat.

"See you in a bit, Grams."

"Be careful, dear," she called as I darted out the back door. Once I reached the barn, Hezzie's ears perked up. I patted his neck. "Let's go for a ride." He stomped his hooves with excitement and followed me out of the pen.

My eyes landed on Liam's pallet. Where would he stay now? For a fleeting moment, I almost curled onto his bed. Instead, I squared my shoulders and grabbed the saddle and other gear off the rack. My plan was to cover as much ground as possible before it got completely dark. I had no idea what to look for. Would the passage be hidden in plain sight? Was it invisible? What would I do if I happened to find it? I probably needed a weapon of some sort, just in case.

I cinched the last buckle on the saddle and glanced around the barn. A horseshoe kit sat on a bench with the extra saddling equipment. Maybe there'd be something in there. I unfolded the leather pouch, finding odd tools strapped to the inside. Most of the tools looked like something out of a horror movie about a deranged dentist. I settled for a small hammer with a sharp point on one end. It wasn't much, but I was sure it could do enough damage if worst came to worst.

I unzipped the top half of my coat and shoved the hammer into my inner pocket. Hezzie glanced at me with a look of judgment.

"Hey, it's the best I can do."

I tugged on my stocking cap and led Hezzie out of the barn. Once outside, I swung into the saddle. With a click of my tongue, we set off in the opposite direction of the clearing. Would Liam be there? If he was, then he wouldn't approve of what I was doing. However, I wasn't his responsibility any longer. It was his decision to leave me. What did he expect me to do? Sit in my room pining for him and feeling completely useless? That was the old Nina. After everything that had occurred within the last few months, I was done crying over a man and waiting to be rescued.

I'd save myself.

I wouldn't have much time to search before it became pitch black. The sun and moon were both present, vying for the right to illuminate the sky. The moon would claim its victory within the next thirty minutes.

I lightly tapped my heels on Hezzie's sides. "Stretch those legs, boy."

He took off, his powerful legs pushing to a speed that I could only dream of being able to run. The chilled air cut through my coat, but I didn't care. The world was perfect while on Hezzie's back.

We would start off by exploring a few miles beyond the barn. It was extremely doubtful that the passage would be near the farm, but it was possible. Could the passage be a house? Some kind of portal? If so, it could be anywhere.

Over the next half hour, Hezzie and I passed dozens of balding trees, a creek, rabbits and squirrels, but nothing resembling a passage. Or at least nothing that I imagined would be similar to a passage. Hezzie's gallop soon became little more than a trot. It was time to call it quits for the day. Unfortunately, I wasn't ready to go home.

I didn't want to see Papa's fragile, pale frame sitting in his chair. Or watch Grams fret in the kitchen to keep her mind off Papa's cancer. I didn't blame her though. That was exactly what I was doing. Keeping myself busy to not have to think about Papa's uncertain future. But mostly because I knew that once I got inside my bedroom, the tears would inevitably fall over Liam.

The farm was a couple of miles away yet. Maybe I'd take my time getting back. Liam would be disappointed in me if he knew I was out here alone at night. But again, I wasn't his problem any longer.

I puffed up my cheeks and blew the air out slowly. Hezzie seemed to do the same thing as his lips quivered. His body trembled beneath me as well. The temperature had dropped drastically. I hadn't even realized how cold it'd become. My teeth chattered and my chin became numb.

Hezzie suddenly stopped. He swung his head from side to side as though searching for something. Couldn't be a snake. I knew from experience he'd be rearing back and hightailing it out of there.

"What is it, boy?"

His ears folded and a snort rumbled through his nostrils. Exactly how he'd acted when we'd first encountered the clearing so many months ago. Goosebumps sprouted on my arms, and my heartrate rose.

Perhaps it was only a raccoon or a coyote. But I knew better than that. Nothing was ever as simple as that. At least not around here or since I met Liam. A lump lodged in my throat. I swallowed past it and glanced around the vast darkness.

My hands shook as I gripped the reins. "Hezzie, go." He continued to snort and paw the ground but refused to move. "Now, Hezzie." I dug my heels into his sides.

Whatever trance he was in broke, and he took off. We dashed across the field, the wind whipping my hair in my face. My eyes darted all around. It was too dark to see anything. Or anybody.

Relief swept over me when we reached the barn. My body trembled as my adrenaline faded. Hezzie glanced back at me, his own body quivering. Had he seen something?

Perhaps Hezzie and I would stick to our search during daylight hours.

CHAPTER FIFTEEN

THE PAIN AND HEARTBREAK SWEPT OVER me in waves all through the night. I hardly slept. When I did, it was in thirty minute spurts, and I tossed and turned so much that at one point I fell out of bed. Liam had left me. I didn't think he ever would. My head told me to accept it, but my heart wouldn't allow me to. My tears fell in torrents, soaking my pillow. My breath came up short, scaring me with hiccups.

A knock suddenly sounded at the door. I sucked in a deep breath and wiped at my eyes. "Come in," I said, rearranging my blankets.

The door cracked open and Grams' silhouette appeared in the doorway. The hall light shining behind her made her resemble an angel.

"Nina, sweetie, are you okay?"

I cleared my throat. "Of course. Why wouldn't I be?"

She stepped further into the room. "It sounded like you were crying."

Grams and Papa would be able to sleep through a meteor hitting the house, yet she'd heard me crying?

Her mouth twisted to the side as she stared at me. Was it too dark for her to see my blotchy face? Even if she couldn't see that I'd been crying, she sensed that something was going on. She would continue to pry until I told her what was wrong. I wanted to tell her that a demon-like being was after me, I'd been attacked by Carl, and my unearthly boyfriend had ended things. But I couldn't.

I released a sigh. "I'm still pretty shaken from the robbery."

Grams stepped into the room, planting herself down on the edge of my bed. "Of course you are, sweetie. How was it being back today?"

"It was pretty nerve wracking."

"I'm sure that it was. Has there been any sign of Carl?"

I swallowed hard. "Not that I'm aware of."

Grams patted my leg. "I'm sure they'll find him soon."

No, they wouldn't. I didn't have any idea what Liam had done with Carl's body, but I did know they'd never find him. He'd forever be considered a missing person, or a fugitive on the run.

"Perhaps you should quit the bank," Grams suggested. "At least for a while until things settle down."

Should I quit? I'd feel bad leaving Mr. Wright in a bind. As much as I loved having a job that led me steps closer to my independence, not working would allow me more time in my search for the Rogue passage.

I bit at my thumbnail. "Maybe you're right."

Grams reached for my free hand. "I need to apologize."

My brows wrinkled. "What for?"

"With everything that's been going on with your grandpa, I feel like I haven't been there enough for you through everything that's occurred in the last few months."

I gave Grams' hand a gentle squeeze. "You've been here for me more than enough. I wouldn't have gotten through any of this without you. Besides, Papa needs you right now more than I do."

Grams nodded slowly. I didn't need to see her clearly to know her eyes were filling with tears.

"What is it, Grams?"

She sniffled. "I hate seeing him like this. That man has been a work horse since the day I met him. He'd work sunup to sundown, only taking a break to eat. Now, he can barely make it from his chair to the bedroom without needing to rest." She removed her hands from mine, wiping at her face.

"I'm sorry, Grams. Is there anything I can do?"

"Actually, would you want to go with him to his treatment tomorrow? I hate saying it, but I'd like to sit this one out. I don't want him to go alone."

Going wouldn't allow me to do any searching, but I'd at least be able to keep tabs on Papa. Not that my one-hundred-fifteen-pound self could protect him very well if we happened upon a Rogue.

"Sure. I'd be happy to go."

I expected Grams to leave then, but she remained on the bed.

"Is there something else you wanted to talk about?"

"Actually there is." She breathed out a sigh. "When do you think you'll start dating again?"

My stomach leapt. "What?"

"I saw how happy Liam made you this summer. Just because that didn't work out doesn't mean you have to give up on finding love. There are a lot of eligible bachelors around here."

A lump caught in my throat at the mention of Liam. I swallowed past it. "I'm not interested in finding somebody, Grams. I'm perfectly happy being single."

"All right, dear. I just thought I'd ask. If you ever change your mind you let me know. I could set you up with some nice fellas."

"Thanks, Grams."

She patted my leg and rose. "You get some rest." The bedroom door latched silently behind her.

I rolled onto my side, gripping the comforter and pulling it up to my chin. I didn't want anybody else. I wanted Liam. My chest seized as I suddenly realized that Liam may never come back to me. For as long as I lived, I'd never love anybody the way I loved him. I turned my face into my pillow, soaking it with my tears.

CHAPTER SIXTEEN

I WOKE THE NEXT MORNING WITH my eyes stinging. They felt heavy and swollen as though I hadn't slept in weeks. I sat up, rubbing at my eyelids. Perhaps this time I'd drink the coffee that Grams kept trying to get me to drink.

I padded to my window and pulled the curtains aside. A fresh dusting of snow covered the grass and the tops of the trees. A shiver shook my body. I pulled on a pair of jeans crumpled on the floor and put on a sweater. On my way to the kitchen, I threw my hair into a ponytail.

Like every morning, Grams was in a tizzy getting breakfast ready. Lately, she made more than her usual bacon and eggs. Pancakes and French toast became a staple in hopes that one of the items would be more appealing to Papa than plain oatmeal. No such luck this morning. He sat at the dining table with his shoulders hunched, stirring the oats around in his bowl. Seemed Grams had given up on trying to get him to eat a heartier breakfast. Papa's nose scrunched as he lifted the spoon to his mouth. Little by little he nibbled off what was piled on his spoon.

Grams glanced at me, lifting her shoulders in a dejected shrug. I shot her a pitiful smile, then joined Papa at the table.

He looked at me briefly. "Good morning." He did a double take. "Have you been crying?"

I hadn't seen myself in a mirror yet. How bad did I look?

Grams set an array of breakfast items in front of me, giving me a sympathetic smile.

"Maybe a little," I said with a sniff. "I need to call the bank

LOVE'S SACRIFICE

and let them know I won't be coming in today. Or any other day for that matter."

"You're quitting? How come?" Papa asked over the top of his coffee mug.

I shot him a wide-eyed look, hoping he'd get the hint. He must have as he swallowed and set his mug down, giving me a slight nod.

I rose from the table and grabbed the receiver on the wall. My fingers shook as I dialed Mr. Wright's cell. I didn't want to quit. But I needed to. Not only for my own safety, but for my grandparents' as well. I wanted to be as close as possible should they need me. Hopefully now that Liam wasn't associated with me, I'd no longer be a target. Still, I couldn't risk anything happening to my grandparents.

Mr. Wright picked up with a hoarse voice as though he'd been asleep.

"Hi, Mr. Wright. It's Nina."

He released a long sigh. "You're quitting on me, aren't you?"

"I'm so sorry."

"Can't say that I blame you. Not with everything that's occurred the last few days."

"Thank you for everything, Mr. Wright."

"Hey, if you ever want to come back you know where to find me."

"I appreciate that. You take care."

"You too."

We hung up and I puffed up my cheeks, letting the air out slowly from my pursed lips. I reclaimed my spot at the table. Grams patted my shoulder and resumed her cooking at the stove.

"Looks like I'll never be leaving you guys. You okay with me living here for the rest of my life?"

Papa's lips lifted, his frown lines disappearing momentarily. "We were hoping you would."

Even though my heart was broken, Papa's words made it

85

flutter with hope.

"Since I have the day off, I thought I'd go with you to the doctor."

Papa glanced at Grams. "You all right with that?"

"Of course, dear."

Papa turned his gaze back to me. "Then I'm happy to have ya."

"I'll go take care of the horses real quick, then we can head out."

I grabbed a piece of bacon, nibbling on it as I headed to the stable. A twinge attacked my stomach as I thought back to the first time Liam tried bacon. He'd looked adorable as his eyes brightened while he gobbled the strips.

Great, a simple thing like bacon reminded me of Liam. How was I going to get through each day when a million reminders would be thrown in my face? I stopped in front of the stable — the biggest reminder of them all. So many memories in this place.

It was in this barn that Liam first used his healing ability on me. I'd sliced my arm so bad I was sure it needed stitches. But Liam healed it within a matter of seconds, leaving me speechless.

I glanced at my forearm, smiling as I trailed my finger along the unblemished skin. He'd healed me multiple times after that due to my constant clumsiness. But it wasn't my physical injuries that I remember him healing the most. He'd repaired my broken heart.

For years, Jeremy had slowly crushed it. Liam had pieced it back together through his unconditional love and respect for me. Now it was breaking all over again.

Tears pooled in my eyes. I took a deep breath and blinked them away.

The stable door seemed to take more strength than usual to slide open. My eyes landed on Liam's pallet. I'd forever see the look on his face as he sat on those hay bales, watching me do my chores with love pouring from his expression. I forced myself to look away.

"Nina," a soft, feminine voice said behind me.

Butterflies assaulted my stomach, and I spun around. A beautiful, life-sized Barbie stood before me.

Kimmie. What was she doing here?

My eyes narrowed slightly. She either didn't notice or didn't care as she smiled so sweetly that I couldn't help but give her a smile in return.

"What can I do for you, Kimmie?" Had Liam sent her?

She shoved her golden locks behind her ears. "Liam doesn't know that I'm here. I'm supposed to be off searching for the passage. I am, but I took a little detour."

"Why?"

Her blue eyes glittered. "To tell you that Liam loves you."

I frowned. I already knew that. Why did she feel the need to come tell me? "What makes you say that?"

"Because of a Martyr's ability to feel the emotions of their assignments, we are also able to feel the emotions of other Martyrs. Only we feel them more strongly." She closed her eyes briefly. "When Liam came back to the clearing last night, his emotions rolled off him so powerfully that they nearly knocked me over."

I swallowed over the lump in my throat. "What was he feeling?"

"Guilt was the strongest. Followed by a sadness that I've never experienced before. But in the midst of all of it, his love for you was undeniable."

Those stupid tears made a comeback. I wouldn't allow myself to cry in front of Kimmie.

"Martyrs automatically feel unconditional love for their assignments when we're placed. Liam feels that love for you tenfold." She smiled sympathetically. "He's only trying to protect you. It's what we do best."

I cleared my throat. "I know. But it doesn't make it hurt any less."

"I understand. He's hurting just as much as you."

A lone tear betrayed me and rolled down my cheek. I wiped it away with the back of my hand. "Will you look after him, please?" My voice cracked.

"Of course. But you must look after yourself as well. It would kill Liam if anything happened to you."

I allowed the tears to fall freely then. Kimmie reached for me, placing her hand on my shoulder. The warmth of her skin soaked through my sweater and through to my flesh. My erratic heart slowed. My breathing evened.

"Everything will be okay, Nina."

I closed my eyes and nodded slowly. When I opened them, Kimmie was gone.

CHAPTER SEVENTEEN

MY THOUGHTS WERE DISTRACTED AS I drove Papa to Beloit for his chemo treatment. A horde of emotions vied for my attention. Guilt for my initial sour attitude towards Kimmie. Sadness over no longer having Liam in my life. Fear for Liam and the other Martyrs on their quest to find the Rogue passage. Finally, worry for Papa and if he'd be healed.

I glanced at Papa out of the corner of my eye. Each bump in the road caused him to wince. I swerved to miss the potholes as much as I could, but Old Blue's rusty suspension made even the smallest dip in the road feel like a cavern.

"You're being awfully quiet, sweet pea."

"So are you."

He smiled lightly. "My excuse is I'm in pain."

"So is mine," I whispered. The rumble of the truck's engine made it so Papa couldn't hear me. I didn't want him to anyway. My heartache was merely a nuisance compared to Papa's chronic agony.

I couldn't continue to feel sorry for myself. Papa and Grams needed me. And if I was going to keep searching for the passage, I needed a clear head.

"How's Liam doing?" Papa asked.

My heart sank. I didn't want to tell him. Not about Carl attacking me last night or Liam breaking up with me. Papa would only worry about me. He didn't need that added stress.

"He's staying busy with his task."

"And are you keeping your word and staying out of it?"

I hated lying to him. But I had to. "Yes."

"Good girl."

I flipped on the radio to keep Papa from asking more questions. One of my favorite bands, Need to Breathe, played over the speakers as they sang about God's love. I had yet to pray for peace about my broken heart. My faith was still rocky, and praying didn't come easily. But I was getting there. I hoped that eventually praying would be the first thing I did when faced with a hard situation, or when I was hurting.

I filled my lungs with air slowly.

Dear Lord, I understand why Liam had to leave me. Please help it to not hurt so badly. Help me to focus on helping Papa today and not on my own selfish needs. And please keep Liam safe.

Papa reached over and placed his hand atop mine. The combination of my short prayer and Papa's simple gesture calmed my heart the same way Liam's peculiar power made me relax.

How I adored my papa. He and Grams were the best things to ever happen to me. I often wondered what my mother would be like if she were still alive. A combination of my grandparents' qualities would make one amazing human being. What would my life have turned out like if she'd been part of raising me? I doubt I would have ended up with a man like Jeremy.

Was she in heaven watching me right now? Did she and my dad get together to talk about me? I hoped they weren't disappointed in me. Surely I'd done some things right to make them proud.

Papa and I rode the remainder of the way trying to stay warm with Old Blue's shoddy heater. Papa hummed along with the radio and I attempted to sing. It was peaceful. My heart still hurt, but it wasn't as debilitating.

We reached the small town of Beloit, but it was a grand city compared to Despair. It took more than a minute to get across and there was more than one stoplight.

"Turn here," Papa said, pointing down a street to the right.

90

My heart leapt as I turned onto the road. In the middle of a large lot, yellow caution tape surrounded a pile of charred wreckage. A stone sign in the yard read Friends' Baptist Church. Below the name were the words "For our God is a consuming fire." Goosebumps spread across my already cold arms. Had that Bible verse been placed there before or after the fire?

Papa craned his neck to continue to look as I passed the scene. He turned around and shook his head. "Unbelievable. How could somebody do something like that? Some people are truly evil."

That they were. And the person who committed such a heinous act could have been anybody. A neighbor, a friend, perhaps even a member of that very church. The enemy could get hold of anybody willing to open their heart to the ways of evil.

Papa released a sigh. "The clinic is just up here."

I pulled into the parking lot of a simple brick building with an abundance of plants surrounding the exterior. Once I found a spot, I turned off Old Blue. Papa didn't make a move to get out, so I continued to sit as well.

"I'm getting real tired of this," he mumbled.

"I know, Papa," I whispered.

He glanced at me. "You sure you want to come in with me? It's not a pretty sight."

"Of course. I can't let you go in alone."

Papa took a deep breath. "Let's go then."

We exited the truck and walked through the entrance together. Our shoes squeaked across the linoleum floor as we approached the receptionist's desk.

The young woman sitting behind the counter gave Papa a toothy grin as she slid a sign-in sheet in front of him. "Hi, Stephen. How are you doing today?"

Papa scrawled his name on the paper. "As well as can be expected."

The receptionist continued to smile. She was probably

trained to stay happy since most of the people who came in were anything less than joyful. "Go on back," she said, hooking her thumb toward a door behind her. Papa shuffled his feet in the direction she indicated. I followed behind, watching his shoulders slump more and more the closer we got to the door.

We opened the door and stepped into a room about the size of the farmhouse kitchen and living room combined. The fluorescent lights overhead shone so bright I had to squint. Along the wall across from us were a dozen brown leather chairs, each separated by a white curtain. Beside each chair was a machine attached to an IV pole.

Only one of the chairs was occupied. A middle-aged woman wearing a headscarf to cover up what I could only assume was a bald head had her eyes closed. The woman's colorless face looked so weary.

I glanced at the IV taped to the inside of her arm, which led to the machine beside her chair. What type of cancer did she have? How many times had she been here? Was the chemotherapy helping?

The woman opened her eyes, and her gaze landed on me. My cheeks reddened when I realized she caught me staring. Instead of glaring at me like I thought she would, she shot me a sweet smile.

"Leukemia," she said.

"Excuse me?"

"I'm sure you're wondering what kind of cancer I have. It's Leukemia."

What did one say to that? I'm sorry didn't seem to quite cut it. Thankfully, Papa interjected so that I didn't have to think of something to say. "Jenny has been doing this for months," he said, settling into one of the chairs.

Jenny released a loud sigh. "Too many months if you ask me. The cancer cells don't seem to think so." She shrugged. "You must be Nina. Your grandfather talks about you all the time."

"All good things I hope."

"Nothing but."

I looked to Papa. The tops of his ears blazed red.

A nurse in bright blue scrubs approached us then. Her curly red hair and freckles made her resemble a slightly older Raggedy Ann. She even had the rosy cheeks. She looked young enough to be in high school.

"Good morning, Stephen," she said, patting his shoulder. She looked at me, offering a grin. "This must be Nina."

"How much do you talk about me, Papa?"

He started to open his mouth, but the nurse interrupted. "When he isn't talking about the farm, he's talking about you."

My heart soared with love for my sweet grandfather. "He's a pretty special guy, isn't he?"

The nurse nodded. "That he is."

"I second that," Jenny declared without opening her eyes.

Papa shifted in his seat. His ears turning to an even deeper shade of red. "All right ladies. Cool it."

"Fine, we'll stop embarrassing you." The nurse turned to me. "I'm Karilyn."

Papa smiled at the young nurse. "Karilyn here is fresh out of nursing school, yet she's the best one."

She rolled her eyes. "I'm sure you say that to all the nurses."

I giggled. "It's nice to meet you. Is it okay if I sit with him?"

"Of course. Pull up a chair." She motioned across the room to a cluster of plastic chairs.

I grabbed one and set it off to the side, slightly facing Papa. Papa placed his right arm on a small table jutting out of the chair and rolled up the sleeve of his flannel shirt. Tears sprang to my eyes at the sight of bruises running up and down his forearm.

Papa looked to me. "The nurses have a hard time finding a vein sometimes. But not Karilyn. She always gets one on the first try."

Karilyn tapped the soft tissue in the crook of Papa's arm. "They call me the vein whisperer."

I winced as she stuck his arm with the IV.

"It doesn't hurt anymore, sweet pea. I've gotten used to it."

Karilyn stretched tape across the IV and pressed a couple buttons on the machine it was hooked up to. "You're all set. I'll check on you in a little bit." She patted Papa on the shoulder and went to the nurses' desk.

Papa released a long sigh and rested his head on the back of the chair. How was he feeling? Would he get sick during the session?

He peeked open one eye. "I'm sure you have a lot of questions. Feel free to ask."

"Can you feel the medicine running through your body?"

"No, I just feel the side effects. Fatigue and nausea."

"Do you usually get sick?"

"Yes." He pointed to a bucket on the floor. "You may need to hand me that after a while."

I couldn't believe that after months of multiple chemo sessions, this was the first time I'd gone. I'd been so busy wallowing in my own grief. The longer I stayed with my grandparents, the more I learned about myself. And there were so many things I didn't like. My selfishness being one. I wasn't the only person going through something. How many people came in and out of this room each day? How many of them were cured as a result of the chemo?

I glanced at Jenny who was growing paler by the minute. She wore a wedding band. Did she also have kids? The people who came in here were fighting for their lives. And here I was heartbroken because my boyfriend broke up with me. Dwelling over what I couldn't change wasn't going to help my grandparents and wasn't going to help the Martyrs' current cause.

I squared my shoulders and took a deep breath. Everything was going to be okay. I had to believe that. Otherwise, what was

I fighting for?

CHAPTER EIGHTEEN

LIAM STARED UP AT THE GLITTERING stars as he lay in the grass of the clearing. Nina was constantly on his mind, and being in their spot only intensified the ache in his heart. It'd been three days since he saw her. Since he did the hardest thing he'd ever had to do. Dying for her was easier than this. The pain in her eyes as he told her he couldn't be with her any longer haunted him daily. But if hurting her was what he had to do to keep her safe, then he'd do it all over again.

After leaving her the other night, he'd buried Carl's body miles from the farm. Then he spent the rest of the evening experiencing so many emotions that he thought he'd go insane. The other Martyrs had tried using their shared power of calming emotions, but it apparently didn't work on each other. He'd paced, he'd cried, he'd raged until he collapsed and fell into a fitful sleep. He woke the next morning with even more determination to stop the Rogues.

He and the others had had no luck yet in finding the passage. It could be anywhere. The search began in Beloit since that was where the crimes originated. They would work their way from there to Despair. They'd trespassed more times than he cared to admit. Homes, churches, stores, but there weren't any indications, such as a lingering smell of vinegar, that Rogues were continually present in those locations.

Movement to his right made Liam jerk his head. Violet sat cross legged, picking daisies and creating some sort of hair piece. She may have been placed on Earth with the appearance of a young girl, but her mind was supremely wise. Even though she couldn't communicate with her voice, her insights spoke volumes.

Liam's gaze landed on Damian who sat on a rock near the pond. The man had been coming to Earth for fifty years to visit his assignment, who was now an old man as well and not in good health. Once his assignment would pass away, he'd no longer be able to come back to Earth.

The trees rustled and Kimmie appeared, returning from a visit with Lulu. Liam had learned that normally Kimmie visited her once a week before Lulu's parents awakened. They'd spend their couple of hours talking, reading stories, and playing. Since being free from the two-hour regulation, Kimmie had been visiting Lulu every day. Whenever Kimmie returned, she appeared in higher spirits than usual. Liam knew how that was. Whenever he visited Nina, he felt refreshed and as though his heart could beat stronger.

Kimmie waved to Violet and Damian before heading in Liam's direction. Crazy how Nina had been jealous of Kimmie. Jealousy wasn't something Martyrs felt naturally. It was a strange sensation to feel it through Nina.

Kimmie sat beside him.

"How's Lulu?" Liam asked.

"She's doing well. Still having nightmares from time to time. But each day is getting better."

Liam had a hard time forgiving himself for not being there sooner the night Jeremy attacked. He'd even had a dream the night before Jeremy came. He'd known it was a sign. He should have trusted his instincts. Instead he'd respected Nina's wishes to stick around the farm to look after her grandparents. If he'd looked after Nina instead, would the outcome have been different? He could have gotten Lulu to safety so that she wouldn't have witnessed the horrific scene that unfolded that night.

"Stop blaming yourself, Liam," Kimmie said.

He glanced in her direction. "It's hard not to."

"Lulu's tough. She'll get through this."

He nodded slowly.

"She asks about Nina frequently, wondering why she doesn't visit her anymore."

Liam ran his hand through his hair. "She blames herself as well."

"Understandable. But it wasn't her fault either. Nina needs to forgive herself." She paused. Her eyes focused on his. "Liam, you need to forgive yourself."

Liam shifted, resting his elbows on his knees. Perhaps someday he'd be able to. For now, his main concern was finding that passage.

"No luck this evening?" Kimmie asked.

He shook his head. "Not even a hint. We investigated the locations of the fires again. Still no clues."

"When was the last fire?"

"Almost a week ago."

Kimmie nodded. "They're being extra careful since they know we're here."

A twig snapped in the surrounding trees, and all four Martyrs came to their feet in a blur. They moved back to back in a huddle, scanning the trees, ready for anything. Liam's heart raced as he stood his ground. Was it a Rogue? Perhaps Nina? Or simply an animal?

A deer suddenly stepped through the trees and into the clearing, unaware of the group. The four of them took a collective breath and stepped away from each other.

"Whose turn is it to take watch?" Kimmie asked.

Liam raised his hand. He wasn't going to get any sleep anyway. Might as well be useful.

I STARED AT THE little boy in the painting. As always, his frown deepened. I prepared myself for his warning. He opened his mouth to yell, but no sound came from his lips. My brows wrinkled, and his eyes widened with fear.

He glanced behind him, and when he turned back around, the right side of his face warped as though water had been splashed on the painting. It wasn't long before the other side of his face began to droop. The boy continued with his soundless screams. Was he screaming in pain? Or out of fear?

I squinted as something started to form in the right corner of the picture. What was it? A red and orange object grew, inching closer to the boy. The boy's face contorted into a mask of fear right before his features seemed to melt before my eyes. Wait! Was that what was happening?

The object was fire! I grabbed hold of the picture frame. With a gasp, I ripped my hands away. I glanced down at my blistered palms.

"Help me!" The boy screamed.

I jerked my head back to the painting. He was no longer there. Instead, flames licked out of the picture, reaching for me like the tentacles of an octopus. Heat swept over me and breathing became difficult. I stepped back, stumbling against the mirror behind me.

"Nina," a voice hissed in my ear.

I closed my eyes. *Wake up, Nina!*

I shot out of bed just before the flames could engulf me. My chest heaved, and despite the chill in my room, sweat trickled down my temples. I clutched my chest and sucked in deep breaths, waiting for my heart to slow.

Why was this dream different? Every other night, it'd been a copy of the night before. And why was I still having them? If they truly were a way that the Rogue leader was trying to get Liam, why would they continue if Liam was no longer in my life? And surely the fire was present only because of the recent arsons. The events were on my mind. That was all.

I glanced at my clock. Three in the morning. I couldn't allow myself to go back to sleep should the dream continue. How would I occupy my time until my grandparents woke?

Leaning over, I flipped on the lamp at my bedside table. I rubbed at my eyes as they adjusted to the light. The Bible on the table caught my eye. I'd placed it there as a dream catcher, but it didn't seem to be working. Since Papa was too tired to read aloud from the word each evening, Grams had taken over, but I hadn't read from the Bible myself in years.

I snatched it up, running my hands over the leather-bound cover. When people read from this book, how did they choose what to read? Did they start from the beginning and read it like a novel? Or pick a page at random? Shrugging, I turned to what I assumed was the table of contents. I trailed my fingers down the list. Genesis, Numbers, Deuteronomy. What in the world did Deuteronomy mean? I stopped at Proverbs. A painting that hung in the living room had a verse from Proverbs scrolled across the bottom. Maybe that would be a good place to start.

Grams always spoke of how God used verses to speak to her. How did she know that it was God speaking to her? What did it make her feel? Would I be able to feel something as well?

I began reading, waiting for a verse to jump out at me. By chapter three, nothing was resonating with me. Wait, what did that one say? *Trust in the Lord with all your heart and lean not on your own understanding, in all your ways acknowledge him, and he will direct your paths.*

My heart suddenly tightened and tears sprang to my eyes. God saw me through the situation with Jeremy, He wouldn't forsake me now. I had to trust that He would see me through this as well.

CHAPTER NINETEEN

AFTER HOURS OF READING THE BIBLE, a new peace settled over my heart. I knew the pain would still be present, but I'd suffered so much worse. For the first time in a long time, I felt like everything was going to be okay. I didn't have all the answers. I didn't know what was going to happen, but with God I could get through anything.

The sun peeked through my curtains, signaling it was time to be productive. I set the Bible on the bedside table and changed into warmer clothes. I had a full day of searching ahead of me. Maybe I needed to find a map of the area. That way I could mark off the spots I'd already surveyed.

I left my bedroom and went straight to the kitchen. Neither of my grandparents were in their usual spots. I spun around, looking into the living room. Papa sat in his chair, shaking his head as he stared at the television. Grams sat on the couch, a handkerchief at her lips as tears rolled down her cheeks. My stomach leapt. Oh, no. What now?

I joined them in the living room, neither seeming to notice I'd entered the room. The news played on the TV screen. The same reporter looked wearier than before as she relayed the most recent events. Live images flashed on the screen in the corner where angry flames blazed from a barn that looked similar to ours. Firefighters held large hoses, spraying streams of water toward the fire.

"I'm now getting reports that the horse is among one of the fatalities," the reporter said.

"There are other fatalities?" I whispered.

Grams nodded slowly. "The homeowner. He tried rescuing the horse." Her voice cracked and she covered her eyes with the handkerchief.

The newscaster looked right into the camera. "Police are treating this as arson and suspect it is connected to the fires in Beloit."

"Where's that fire?" I asked.

"Just outside of Despair," Papa grumbled. "Not far from here."

Grams wiped a tear from her cheek. "You've met the Hendricks family at church, dear."

I closed my eyes. Was it the same Rogue setting these fires? Or a group? How many Rogues were out there?

My eyes popped open, and my nostrils flared. The crimes were spreading. We had to stop this. Before they destroyed all of Despair. It was time to get busy.

I sprang from the couch and headed for the kitchen.

"Where you going, sweet pea?" Papa asked.

Uh-oh. He knew something was up. Why did he have to be so intuitive?

I turned around, trying not to make my real intentions apparent on my face. "For a quick ride."

Grams made a move to stand. "Let me make you something to eat."

I held out my palm. "It's okay Grams. I'm not that hungry."

I turned back around.

"Sweet pea?"

Stopping in the kitchen doorway, I glanced over my shoulder. "Yes, Papa?"

He was silent for a beat, grinding his lips together. What was he going to say? Forbid me from going anywhere?

He released a sigh. "Be careful."

Ever the protector. He had an idea of what I was going to do.

And he didn't want me to do it. But we were both stubborn. Neither of us would win that battle. "I'll be safe," I said with a smile.

I went to the back porch, slipping on my boots and coat. After my ride last night, I realized a more effective weapon was sorely needed. The only gun I had access to was Papa's shotgun. But that would be rather difficult to carry inconspicuously while riding Hezzie. Perhaps Papa had something in the shed behind the house.

I remained on guard on the quick jaunt to the backyard. In front of the shed, the fishing boat sat covered with a tarp. The memory of the day Liam and I went to the lake with my grandparents flashed through my mind. My heart threatened to remind me of my pain, but I shook it off.

I opened the shed door, greeted by the smell of old grass and pine. I reached up, finding the string to turn on the bulb hanging overhead. The light lit up the space, revealing the riding lawn mower and gardening equipment, including an axe. How heavy was an axe? Maybe that would make a good weapon.

The rusty thing didn't look too hefty. I grabbed hold of the wooden handle and lifted. And set it right back down. Either I was a major weakling or that axe was made of lead.

Planting my hands on my hips, I glanced around for something else. My eyes landed on a pegboard speckled with tools. Wrench, screwdriver, hammer, hatchet. Aha! A hatchet. A mini axe was exactly what I needed.

I maneuvered my way around the lawnmower to the tools. I gripped the hatchet, turning it every which way. It was much easier to hold than the axe. Carefully, I slid my finger over the sharp edge. Yep, it would do in a pinch. I shoved the handle into the back of my jeans beneath my shirt. The cold metal against my skin made shivers run up and down my body.

Now for a map. I bit at my thumbnail. Where could I find a map? I snapped my fingers. The truck. Surely there was something in there. I turned out the light and closed the door to the shed, heading for Old Blue. I felt safer already having the hatchet within my reach. But even if I needed it, would I be able to hurt someone? Knowing they were being controlled by a Rogue would make it hard to do so. However, if my life or somebody else's was being threatened, I wouldn't hesitate to act.

I crawled into the passenger side of the truck and opened the glove compartment. Half-a-dozen candy bar wrappers poured out and littered the floor.

"Goodness, Papa." No wonder he once had such a pot belly. I shoved aside the remaining candy wrappers, revealing the car manual. I lifted the book. Bingo! A handheld Atlas.

I opened it up, only to find the maps so tiny that my grandparents would certainly need a magnifying glass to see them. Each state map included a series of county maps. Thankfully, that included the county Despair was in. I was no Magellan, but if I knew cross streets, then I'd be able to pin point my location.

Squinting, I trailed my index finger along the county map, finding the dirt road my grandparents' farm sat on. There was so much land I had yet to explore. It may have been scary not knowing what I might find while doing my search, but it was also exciting knowing I would see parts of the area surrounding Despair I'd never experienced before. Some areas I would explore on foot, some by horse, and others by truck. It would keep me busy. Busy enough to hopefully keep my mind off the pain that had since faded to a dull ache.

104

CHAPTER TWENTY

ONCE THE HORSES HAD BEEN FED, I readied Hezzie and tried to not let Hazel guilt trip me into taking her instead. Armed with the hatchet and a small map, I swung onto Hezzie's back. Since I no longer had a job or Liam to take up my time, I wasn't on any kind of schedule. Hezzie and I could roam the land all day if we wanted to.

The first area I set off to explore led behind the Nelsons' property. I steered Hezzie to take the long way, giving the clearing a wide berth. Not only did I want to avoid it in case the Martyrs were gathered there, it also held too many memories. And I didn't want or need any distractions.

I squared my shoulders and took a deep breath. The cold air burned my lungs but was also strangely refreshing. It was barely November. If it was this cold already, what would winter be like?

Hezzie's heavy hooves crunching on the dead grass and the whistle of the wind were the only sounds to be heard. The country was such a peaceful place. Hard to believe I used to prefer the city. I'd become a completely different person in the last few months. Of course, there were still issues I was working through, but it was by God's grace that I was still here. Perhaps this was my purpose. To help bring down the Rogues.

I shook my head, trying to focus my mind. Complete awareness was necessary at the moment. Anything out of the ordinary could be a clue. But how big could the passage be? Did the Rogues pass through in the mist form that rose from Carl? If so, then the passage could be as small as a crack in the ground.

Was this mission as crazy as looking for a needle in a haystack? Every tree we passed, I searched for a peculiar notch. Each tall area of grass, I combed through for evidence. After dismounting for the fourth time to investigate what turned out to be yet another snake hole, Hezzie gave an exasperated quiver of his lips.

"My thoughts exactly, buddy. Maybe I'm in over my head." We'd wandered far enough that the Nelsons' house could be seen. A dozen sparse trees stood between me and the beautiful colonial home that now appeared to me as something out of a horror movie. How could they stand to still live there?

A pain clutched my chest. I used to check on Lulu, but I couldn't remember the last time I had. At church, I avoided the Nelsons as much as possible. I think they avoided me as well, but that could have been in my head due to my own insecurities.

My eyes landed on the storm shelter in the backyard. How long had Lulu been in that dark underground hole? Had it been minutes? Hours? When I replayed the events of that night, the timeline was such a blur. I could only imagine the fear she'd felt as Jeremy snatched her from her bed and threw her in that shelter. How scared she must have been as the storm raged outside, crying for her parents to get her.

A tear squeezed out of the corner of one eye and trailed down my cheek. Hezzie nosed my shoulder. I turned to him, stroking the spot between his eyes. "I'm okay, buddy."

Just then, a joyous squeal sounded from the direction of the Nelson home. A little boy ran down the back steps and out into the backyard. Kevin Jr. had grown so much in the last few months.

"Kevin Jr., you get back in here and put your coat on!" Ruthie yelled from the back door.

A curly headed blonde girl squeezed through her mother's legs and dashed out toward her little brother.

"You too, Lulu!" Ruthie called.

Lulu giggled as she tackled Kevin to the ground. I couldn't

help but smile. It was nice to see that she could still have happy moments. Maybe I hadn't ruined her life after all.

I grabbed hold of Hezzie's reins. "We better go before they see us." I turned, leading Hezzie away.

"Nina?" A small voice called to me.

My shoulders rose and I winced. With a deep breath, I turned back around.

Lulu ran toward me as fast as her little legs could go. Once she was close, she leapt at me, slamming her body against mine and wrapping her arms around my neck. The unexpected force knocked me backward, and I fell to the ground with Lulu on top of me.

"Lulu!" Ruthie's voice was closer than it'd been moments before.

Lulu rested her head on my chest. "I missed you," she mumbled.

I draped my arms over her tiny frame, hugging her to me. "I've missed you, too."

Ruthie suddenly stood over us with Kevin Jr. on her hip. "Oh my goodness, Nina. I am so sorry. Are you okay?"

I nodded into Lulu's hair.

Lulu lifted her head, her blue eyes looking directly into mine. "Why don't you ever come see me anymore?"

Her words were like a punch in my stomach. I swallowed hard to keep my tears from welling. "I'm sorry, Lulu." For what happened to her that night. For not making an effort to reach out to her more.

Lulu squeezed me tight. "It's okay."

I glanced up at Ruthie. She smiled through the tears glistening in her own eyes.

A weight seemed to lift from my shoulders. I hadn't realized I was carrying around so much guilt. I suddenly felt lighter and stronger. Amazing how somebody's forgiveness could be so freeing.

"Do you want to come inside?" Lulu asked.

I looked to Ruthie. She nodded while wiping at her eyes.

I grinned at Lulu. "I'd love to." The search could wait.

Lulu climbed off me and grabbed my hand, helping me to my feet.

I tied Hezzie's reins to a branch nearby and patted his side. "Be back in a bit."

Ruthie led the way to her house, with Lulu skipping ahead momentarily before coming back to join us. Excitement seemed to course through her veins as she hopped from one foot to the other. But the closer we got to the Nelsons' home, the faster my heart raced. How would it feel to set foot in the scene of the crime?

I followed the family through the back door, trying to not let the memories invade my thoughts. I was successful as we walked through the kitchen. But then we reached the entryway. The image of Jeremy kicking me in the ribs as I lay on the floor flashed in my mind. Then he pushed me against the wall, nearly strangling me to death until I smashed a lamp over his head. The sight of blood pooling beneath him, saturating the floor was still so vivid. A rug now spread across the wood where he'd lain. Was it because the crime scene cleaners couldn't get all the blood out? My stomach churned at the thought.

Lulu grabbed my hand, bringing me back to the present. She led me to the living room, plopping down on the couch and patting the space beside her for me to join. I sat next to her on the sofa.

"Can I get you anything to drink? Coffee? Hot chocolate?" Ruthie said.

"Hot chocolate would be fantastic. Thank you."

Ruthie headed to the kitchen with Kevin Jr. still on her hip.

Lulu leaned into me. "Kimmie came to see me yesterday," she whispered.

I craned my neck to make sure Ruthie was indeed in the kitchen, then turned back to Lulu. I lowered my voice. "I met

Kimmie."

Lulu's bright eyes widened. "You did? Isn't she pretty?"

"She's beautiful." Surprisingly my jealousy didn't make an appearance.

"She said she's helping Liam with something."

I nodded. "Did she tell you what she was helping him with?"

Lulu shook her head. "No, but she told me to stay safe and to let her know if I see any bad guys."

"Yes, you have to be very careful Lulu."

Ruthie arrived back in the living room, bringing my conversation with Lulu to an end. She handed me a mug full of steaming cocoa. I took a sip, the contents warming me all the way to my toes.

"This is delicious, Ruthie. Thank you."

She waved her hand. "It's just an instant mix. Nothing special." Kevin Jr. wiggled out of her arms and onto the floor.

"How are you doing?" she asked. The genuine concern in her eyes made me want to weep. I was the one who should be asking how they were all doing.

I shrugged. "I'm okay."

"And your grandfather?"

"He's getting by."

"Lulu prays for him every night."

I looked to Lulu. "Is that right?"

She nodded, the action making her curls bounce into her eyes. She swiped them away. "I pray for you, too."

My heart squeezed. "You do?"

"Yep. And I know God is going to answer my prayers. He's already answered one."

"And what was that?"

"That you'd come see me."

A knot formed in my throat. I should have come to see her long ago. Had she thought I didn't care about her?

"You're welcome here any time, Nina," Ruthie chimed. "I

mean it."

I shot her a smile, trying to hide my tears. How could this family be so loving and forgiving? Their whole world had been turned upside down because of me. How could they even still want to talk to me? Was it their faith that made them that way? I wanted that kind of faith. The kind that made it possible to love no matter what. The same way that Liam and the other Martyrs loved.

Perhaps I'd get there. Someday.

CHAPTER TWENTY-ONE

WHEN I REACHED THE FARM AFTER my visit with the Nelsons, a new peace had settled within my soul. I should have done that a long time ago. If I simply would have had the courage to talk to the sweet family, I could have saved myself a lot of stress. But, it was just like me to learn the hard way.

After putting Hezzie back in the stable, I left the barn with a contented sigh. Life could be tough at times, but God used the little moments to give me perseverance. For that, I was so thankful.

"Nina!" Grams yelled from the back porch. "Hurry!"

My stomach somersaulted. Oh, no. Something happened to Papa.

I ran for the house, but the closer I got I realized Grams was smiling. I reached the porch and Grams grabbed my hands.

My eyes widened. "What? What is it?"

Tears trailed down her rosy cheeks and she laughed. "Papa's doctor just called. The cancer's gone, Nina."

I lifted my brows. "How?"

Papa came up behind her. "By some miracle," he said through a grin.

"His blood test after his recent chemo session showed no sign of cancer," Grams explained. "He'll have to continue with regular doctor visits to be sure it doesn't return, but—"

"This means you're in remission?"

Papa nodded. "It does indeed."

I grabbed his shoulders and pulled him into a hug. Grams wrapped her arms around us both.

Tears filled my eyes. *Thank you, God. Thank you.* God truly was a miracle worker, capable of doing anything. It was past time I started trusting in that.

LIAM COULDN'T HELP HIMSELF. He had to at least check on Nina. He hoped he wouldn't find her inconsolable over him, however, he didn't expect to. She wouldn't let a broken heart keep her from living life. She'd suffered for too long in the past. If he knew her like he thought he did, she would use the heart ache to fuel something else. He only prayed it wasn't trying to find the passage.

He reached the farm around midnight. He longed to go to the stable, fall asleep on his pallet, and wake the next morning to find Nina's beautiful face staring down at him. But those days were over. For now. Would he ever have that again? He shook his head. His mission for the moment was clear. As much as it killed him, he couldn't let the situation with Nina deter him from completing his purpose. However, checking on her couldn't hurt. He only needed to know she was safe and well.

With silent footfalls, he approached Nina's window. The action was so reminiscent of the summer nights that he'd sneak into her bedroom to watch her sleep. A crooked smile crossed his lips as he thought back to how angry she'd been when she found out. How he missed her fiery spirit.

Without a sound, he raised the window and crawled through the opening. A cold breeze followed him, making the sheer curtains dance. He shut the window quickly and turned around to find Nina curled on her side, facing him with her eyes closed. His heart clenched at the sight of her. She was so beautiful it hurt. His fingers twitched at his side as he ached to cup her face and press his lips to hers.

He knelt beside the bed. She looked so serene when she slept. Her brows suddenly creased, and a whimper escaped her lips.

Was she having another nightmare? Surely it wasn't the same one she'd been having. Now that he was out of the picture, the Rogue leader had no use for her. Unless the leader knew he was here.

Liam fisted his hand and banged it lightly against his forehead. It was irresponsible and dangerous for him to come. The leader could still be watching to see if Nina had ties to him.

"I'm sorry I've caused you so much extra pain," he whispered. The least he could do was keep his promise that he'd stay away. If she were to wake, it would only cause her confusion to find him here. He needed to go. But he couldn't leave her to finish the bad dream.

Liam gently placed his hand atop her head. In his mind's eye, he brought forth all his best memories of their time together. Talking and laughing for hours in the clearing, stealing kisses, and simply holding on to each other in contented silence. The memories made his heart ache, yet also flutter with joy. He projected the images from himself to Nina. The crease between Nina's brows softened, and a smile played at her lips. Hopefully when she awakened the dream would be considered pleasant, rather than painful.

Reluctantly, Liam removed his hand from her head. He stared at her for a few more minutes, before finally rising to leave. At the window, he took one last look. *I love you. With all that I am, I love you.* With that last thought, he escaped through the window and back into the night.

WHEN I WOKE THE next morning, I felt more refreshed than I had in days. A smile spread across my face as I remembered Papa was cancer free. And my recurring nightmare hadn't paid me a visit last night. A sadness suddenly settled over my heart as I thought back to the dream I'd had. Liam and I had lounged in the grass as we so often did, simply laughing and enjoying each other's company. Would I ever get to experience that again?

I closed my eyes, ready to start my day differently than usual. *Lord, if it's your will that Liam and I be together, I ask that you allow me to be patient. Please help me to focus on more important things right now. In your son's name, Amen.*

With a deep breath, I climbed out of bed. After changing into jeans and a sweater, I left my room to find Papa and Grams in the kitchen. For once, Papa ate something other than oatmeal. Eggs and bacon, his usual favorite, sat half eaten on his plate. I couldn't help but grin.

"Good morning, sweet pea," Papa said over a mouthful of egg. "What's on your agenda for today?"

I joined Papa at the table. "I thought I'd go for a ride this morning. After that, no plans."

"I don't think you'll be going for a ride. At least not for very long," Grams said.

"Why not?"

"We got a few inches of snow last night."

My brows rose. I pushed up from the table and leaned over the sink to look out the window. Sure enough. The rising sun's rays made the snow-covered ground sparkle like a million diamonds. I wouldn't let a little snow deter me from continuing my search. I'd simply have to bundle up more.

I turned away from the window. "A little snow never hurt anybody. Does Hezzie have snow boots?"

My grandparents shot me a blank stare, trying to decide if I was serious.

"Kidding, guys," I said with a crooked grin.

Papa chuckled. I couldn't remember the last time I'd heard him laugh. He really must be feeling better.

I grabbed a piece of bacon and nibbled on the end. "I won't be out long. Enough to get some fresh air and for Hezzie to stretch his legs." And to do a quick search of another area.

"You can borrow one of my thicker coats, dear," Grams said.

I finished my bacon and headed for the coat closet. Inside, I found a grey down coat with a hood and matching mittens. My body warmed as soon as I slipped into the coat. I passed through the kitchen to the back porch, and as I put on my boots Papa called out to me to be careful.

"Will do, Papa," I called back.

When I walked outside, I used my hand to shade my eyes from the reflection of the sun off the snow. All sound seemed to have been absorbed by the white blanket that covered every inch of anything outdoors.

The ground before me appeared so smooth that I almost hated to disturb it with my foot prints. I stepped down from the stairs, my boot sinking into the powder. Snow in New York was never this lovely since the constant traffic turned it to sludge. This snow was pure and untainted.

I stepped down and tromped through the thick snow, the powder sticking to the bottom of my jeans. My slightly labored breathing was the only sound to be heard. I came up on the stable and stopped in my tracks. A set of human footprints circled around the barn. No other prints led to or from the stable. It was as though whoever created them had simply disappeared.

I spun around, scanning the area. No sign of life. I wrapped my arms around my middle, trying to not jump to conclusions. It could have been Liam simply checking on the horses. I'd stick with that explanation. If I entertained any of the other possibilities swirling around in my head, I'd have a panic attack.

With a deep breath and a quick prayer that I wouldn't find anything out of the ordinary inside the barn, I slid open the door. I flipped on the light and my heart stopped. On the far wall hung the painting of the boy from my dream.

CHAPTER TWENTY-TWO

No. That couldn't be. It couldn't be here.

The boy looked different. What was it? He was smiling. I took a tentative step forward, and his curved lips dropped into a frown. My brows wrinkled. I took another step toward the painting, and bags formed beneath his sad eyes. What would happen to him if I got any closer? With one more stride, I stood face to face with the little boy. His face morphed and contorted as though it were made of wax. It dissolved completely, the paint mixed together into a swirl of red and orange hues. What in the world?

A feeling in the pit of my stomach told me to run. An inner voice begged me to get away. But I couldn't stop watching the strange occurrence unfolding before me. I was mesmerized. The paint colors stopped swirling and separated. A new portrait began to paint itself. It took shape of a woman with soft auburn hair and intoxicating green eyes. It was me. The painting was of me.

I stared at the upgraded version of myself. She was so beautiful with flawless skin. No freckles, no blemishes, no scar at her neck. The contented smile on her face made me experience an envy I never knew I could feel. Why was she so happy?

The whinny of a horse startled me and pulled my attention away from the painting. I clutched my chest. "Hezzie, you scared me!"

I turned back to the portrait. My heart jumped all over again. The painting was gone. I spun around, searching the other barn walls. Nothing. Bare, save for saddle equipment. I closed my eyes and pinched the bridge of my nose. "I really am losing it."

Wait, where's Hazel? My eyes shot open, and I looked to Hazel's empty pen. The door that led to the field was still latched and locked. She couldn't have let herself out. Somebody had to have done it. Whoever's footprints were outside had to be the culprit. Did they steal her? My nostrils flared as rage rolled through my body. But if somebody had stolen her, wouldn't I have seen hoof prints as well? Unless they let her out before it snowed. But then why were their prints in the snow? Did they come back once it had snowed to get Hezzie, but were unsuccessful? None of it made any sense.

"Come on, buddy. We need to find Hazel." I unlocked Hezzie's gate and readied his saddle the quickest I ever had. Before getting onto his back, I grabbed my trusty hatchet and stuck it in the back of my pants. It might come in handy today.

I led Hezzie out of the barn, sliding the door closed behind me. With a hop, I plopped into the saddle, slipped the hood of my coat on my head, and slid my hands into the mittens.

"Let's go," I said, tapping Hezzie's sides. He took off in a sprint, seeming to pick up on the urgency in my voice.

The anger coursing through my veins made me oblivious to the cold surrounding us. I didn't even know where to look for Hazel. Surely Hezzie could sniff her out. Or could only dogs do that? I didn't steer him in any particular direction, only allowed him to go wherever he pleased. I searched for hoof prints, but the only other animal print we encountered was that of a bunny.

After fifteen minutes, my cold nose started to run, and my fingers became numb. Hazel could be anywhere. Hezzie slowed and came to a stop at the trees that we'd ventured into this summer. Where he'd been spooked by a snake and knocked me out of the saddle. Hezzie had taken off, leaving me behind with a concussion and a broken leg. If it weren't for Liam, who knows what would have happened to me.

Hezzie swiveled his neck around to look at me.

"I think we're okay to go in there. I doubt we'll see any snakes this time around. But if we do, please don't do anything drastic. Deal?"

Hezzie's lips quivered as though in agreement. He dipped his head and squeezed through the trees, following the narrow trail. The soft thud of his hooves echoed off the trees. How far did this trail lead? Last time we were here I didn't get very far. From my vantage point, it seemed endless.

A twig snapped to the right. Hezzie stopped and we both turned in the direction of the sound. I held my breath. Perhaps the weight of snow caused a branch to break.

"Keep going, boy. It was probably a rabbit or a squirrel."

Hezzie continued walking, stepping over fallen branches with unfathomable grace. Even though I should have been focusing on looking for the passage and more importantly trying to find Hazel, my mind wandered to thoughts of Liam. I couldn't help but wonder what he was doing at that moment. Surely he was looking for the passage. But in the midst of his search, was he thinking about me?

Another twig snapped. Hezzie stopped once again and our heads swiveled to the left this time. That one had been much louder and closer. It couldn't have been a mere rabbit or squirrel. I squinted against the bright white, finding nothing but trees and snow. Hezzie's ears folded as he snorted.

My heart hammered in my chest. "Maybe we should get out of here, boy."

Another snap, followed by the wickedest laugh I'd ever heard. The cackle came from all directions, reverberating off the trees and making it impossible for me to pinpoint the source. I reached for the hatchet, pulling it from my pants in a death grip.

My eyes darted to the left, to the right, and behind me. "Whoever is out there, I am armed. If you have Hazel, return her to me and nobody has to get hurt."

A few yards away, a dark figure darted from behind one tree to the next with lightning fast speed. I clutched the hatchet tighter, ready to throw it or bring it down on whoever, or whatever, may be out there.

"Niiinnnaaa," a dark voice hissed.

My chest rose and fell on quick inhalations. "What do you want?"

"You." The voice answered directly in my ear.

A scream passed my lips, and I dropped my weapon. I watched it become buried in the snow. "Run, Hezzie!"

Hezzie obeyed, and I clutched his reins as he ran at a ground-eating gallop through the constricted forest. I glanced around wildly, ready for whoever was in the woods to pounce and attack. Who was it? A Rogue? The Rogue leader himself? Why was he still coming after me?

Hezzie squealed and halted, the sudden stop causing my body to propel over his head. I kept my grip on the reins, and closed my eyes as I prepared to slam into the ground. But I didn't. My feet and body hadn't come into contact with anything. My eyes popped open and I looked down. My eyes widened and a scream passed my lips as I stared down into the dark pit I dangled over. The hole was so deep I couldn't see the bottom. It stretched for miles every which way like a canyon.

Tightening my hold on the reins, I looked up. Hezzie's hooves stood on the edge of the cliff. He snorted and stared down at me with large, glassy eyes. I swung my legs carefully, trying to reach the rocky side of the cliff. The tips of my toes slipped and chunks of rock disappeared into the abyss. I wasn't going to be able to get myself out.

Liam! Would he even hear me? Since he'd separated himself from me, had he turned off whatever power he had that made him able to hear me?

My grip on the reins began to slip. I wasn't going to be able to hold on much longer. "Hezzie, pull me up!" I said with a voice filled with such fear that I didn't recognize it as my own.

Hezzie tugged, and I held on for dear life, praying that the bridle would hold. Hezzie dragged me up and out of the crevasse. My feet couldn't find solid ground fast enough. I fell to my knees, then collapsed into the snow. Adrenaline coursed through my body as I sucked in deep breaths. My cheek became numb due to the iciness below it, but I didn't care. I was alive. That's all that mattered.

Hezzie nudged my shoulder with his nose. "I'm okay. Give me a second, boy."

My breathing slowed, as did my heart. Somewhere in the fray I'd lost my mittens. With aching hands, I lifted myself up from the ground. I stood, my back to the pit, staring down at my purple fingers. Could they be frost bitten? I needed to get out of here. What other strange things lay in wait for me out here? Where in the world had that chasm come from?

I turned around and my heart dropped into my stomach. The large hole that I had hung over just moments ago was gone. In its place were sparse trees and snow covered grass.

"What? This can't be," I whispered, glancing around frantically. I looked at Hezzie. "You saw it here, right?" I rested my hands on top of my head. "What is going on?"

My mouth dropped open as realization hit me. It was an illusion. The Rogue leader could cause hallucinations, right? That was the only explanation. A canyon couldn't simply disappear. But my goodness, it had seemed so real. What would have happened if I'd fallen into the depths of something that wasn't really there?

Shivers ran up and down my spine. This leader was far more powerful than I could have imagined. I spun around slowly, my eyes darting suspiciously. What else out here was an illusion? What other type of trickery might I encounter? Maybe I needed to stop searching for the passage. Was that why the leader was still messing with me? Had I gotten myself in too deep and now wouldn't be able to crawl out?

I shook my head. I was done. If the leader could create a hallucination like I'd just experienced, I didn't want to know what else he could do. "Let's go, Hezzie. Hazel will have to find her own way home."

Before climbing back into the saddle, I cupped my hands over my mouth and blew into them. The warm air temporarily thawed my fingers. I scrambled onto Hezzie's back and reined him in the direction we'd come. Only, the trail no longer existed. A thick row of trees stood before us like soldiers guarding a gate.

No, this couldn't be. This wasn't real. It had to be another illusion. Would we be able to pass through it then? I reached out to touch a leaf of one of the trees. The brown, dying foliage felt as rough as any other. I ripped it from the branch, squeezing it in my hand. It crunched in my palm the way a normal leaf would. The trees were tangible.

I squeezed my eyes shut, willing the hallucination to disappear. When I opened them, the trees still stood guard. Going through the trees obviously wasn't an option. We'd have to find another way out.

I turned Hezzie around again. "What in the world? This is ridiculous."

Another row of trees had formed, creating an impenetrable barrier. The only directions to go were either left or right. Both looked to stretch on forever. If I chose a route to travel, would we ever get out?

Liam, I could really use you right now.

I didn't expect him to come. Still, it was worth a shot. I waited a couple of minutes, hoping he'd appear through the trees with that smile meant only for me, ready to rescue me exactly as he had so many times before. But he didn't. Hezzie and I were on our own.

I released a sigh. "Which way, buddy? Left or right?"

Hezzie swiveled his head in both directions, settling for the right. The sun glared into our eyes from that direction. Were we heading east? Or was the sun a hallucination as well?

My mind remained on full alert as we traveled. What dangers could be waiting for us? Would the ground suddenly give way, and we'd plummet to our deaths? Once again, my heartrate rose. My hands shook, whether from the cold or fear I wasn't sure.

We continued for what felt like hours. Long enough for the sun to shine directly overhead. Yet no trail end in sight. Every part of my body ached from exhaustion, but more so from the cold. I could no longer feel my fingers and toes. My teeth chattered to the point that I thought my jaw might fall off.

I'm going to freeze to death out here. Even Hezzie had intermittent tremors.

How long could a hallucination last? Or was this no longer a part of the illusion, and we were simply lost?

God, please get us out of here.

Each tree we passed looked the same as the last. Were we somehow going in circles? I glanced behind us. The trail appeared to be linear, but being out here in isolation surrounded by illusions was making my head spin.

"I . . . don't know . . . if we'll make it . . . out of here, Hezzie." My numb lips could hardly form the words.

Over time, my eyelids grew heavy. My heart seemed to pump blood at an alarmingly slower pace. All I wanted to do was fall asleep.

"You . . . keep walking . . . boy." I leaned forward, resting my cheek against Hezzie's mane. "I'm . . . going to take . . . a little nap."

Hezzie suddenly stopped. I jerked up. Oh, no. What was it now?

A little girl stood in Hezzie's way. Wait, I knew that girl. Violet! I'd recognize that purple hair anywhere. She cocked her head to the side.

I wanted to say so much. What was she doing here? Could she get us out? All I managed to say was, "Help."

Violet stepped forward with such elegance she appeared to be floating. She grabbed hold of the reins, gently pulling them from my hands. She turned Hezzie, steering us toward the never-ending line of trees.

"Wait! You can't go through."

She either didn't care or wasn't listening, because she continued walking. I closed my eyes and lifted my arms, protecting myself from the branches that would inevitably knock me in the face. But nothing happened. Hesitantly, I lowered my arms and opened my eyes. Somehow we'd passed through the trees. I looked behind us. The trees weren't there. Instead, the normal trail where Hezzie and I had started was in their place.

Could we have gone through the hallucination if I'd only set my mind to it? Or did Violet possess the power to allow us to go through? Or perhaps she hadn't even seen the illusion. In any case, I was so thankful she'd come to our rescue. Wait, why was she there?

"Violet, how did you find me?" I realized I could feel my lips once again. And my extremities were beginning to thaw. Had it been colder within the illusion?

She looked at me with a blank stare as she continued leading Hezzie and me out of the woods. Of course she didn't answer. She couldn't talk. Could she at least nod or shake her head? Perhaps yes or no questions would work.

"Were you looking for me?"

A slight shift of her head told me no.

"Were you searching for the passage?"

If I had blinked, I would've missed her nod.

"Have you had any luck?"

A quick shake of her head. Violet turned her attention forward, obviously done with my questions. Would she let Liam know that I'd been out on my own? Hopefully not. I didn't need him to worry about me.

We reached the opening that led out of the woods. Violet released the reins and headed back into the forest.

"Violet!" I called.

She stopped, glancing over her shoulder. Her green eyes remained expressionless. What was going on inside her mind?

"Thank you," I said.

Her mouth lifted into what I thought was a smile, but it disappeared before I could examine it further.

She turned away, and in normal Martyr fashion, disappeared into the woods.

CHAPTER TWENTY-THREE

MY EYES SHIFTED SIDE TO SIDE as we approached the stable. So many things could be a hallucination. Would I even know what was and what wasn't? Was I safe to go anywhere? Was I even safe in the farmhouse?

I dismounted Hezzie and slid open the barn door. The aroma of fresh hay and oats welcomed me. As did Papa and Hazel.

Papa paused brushing Hazel. "Hey, sweet pea. Have a nice ride?"

"Where did you find Hazel?"

Papa's brows wrinkled. "What do you mean?" I pulled Hezzie in behind me. "Hazel wasn't here. Hezzie and I went searching for her."

The look Papa gave me made me feel insane. "She's been here the whole time, Nina. I came out shortly after you and Hezzie left."

My mouth fell open. She'd been here? But, how? It didn't make any sense. Unless . . . had the leader caused me to hallucinate that she wasn't in her pen? How could he do that?

"How long have you been out here?" I asked.

"Not long. Maybe thirty minutes."

How was that possible? I thought I'd been gone for hours. Could a hallucination distort time? I raised a skeptical brow at Papa. What if Papa was a hallucination? He rarely spent time in the barn.

I approached him cautiously as he continued to brush Hazel down. "Why'd you come out here?"

He stopped momentarily to look at me again. "Why am I

getting the fifth degree?"

I shrugged. "Just asking."

"I was going stir crazy in that house. I'm still weak, so I can't do much. Seemed hanging out with Hazel would be harmless."

Okay, that was understandable. Still, I couldn't help but have my doubts. I cocked my head to the side, looking Papa up and down. He sure looked like my Papa. From every freckle on his bald head to each wrinkle on his craggy face. If he was an illusion, then it certainly was a detailed one. If I touched him, would he feel as real as those trees had? I reached out, poking Papa in the neck with my index finger.

Papa swatted at his neck as though a bug had bitten him. He faced me with anger written across his brow. "Ouch! What in the Sam Hill are you doing?"

Well, he felt real. "Sorry, I thought I saw something on your neck."

Papa shot me a skeptical look and moved to the other side of Hazel.

One more test. Could he answer questions only the real Papa would know? Or were the hallucinations created based on my own memories since Rogues could read my thoughts? If I asked a question, would the hallucination be able to dig around in my head for the correct answer? This was all too bizarre. How would I be able to trust anybody if I couldn't tell if they were real?

Perhaps I should ask a question that even I didn't know the answer to, but would be able to find out the answer. I scratched at the back of my head. What type of question would that be? A date for something. I knew Papa's and Grams' birthdays, so that wouldn't work.

I snapped my fingers. "Papa, when is your anniversary?"

"February ninth. Why?"

Without a word, I ran for the house. I could only imagine the look on Papa's face at that moment. An incredulous one to be sure. He was probably wondering once again if I'd gone crazy.

I trudged into the kitchen, my boots tracking in snow. Grams glanced up from folding laundry at the table. Was she really my Grams?

"Take off your shoes please, dear. I just cleaned the floor." She certainly seemed like the real Grams.

I nearly fell over as I slipped off my boots. "What day did you get married, Grams?"

Grams cocked her head to the side. "February ninth. Why do you ask?"

I unzipped and slid off my coat, throwing it on the back of one of the dining chairs. "Do you have your wedding license handy?"

Grams' brows wrinkled. "No, dear. It's in a safety deposit box at the bank."

Right. It would be. "Do you have any wedding photos? I don't think I've ever seen any other than what's in frames around the house."

Papa tromped in behind me, stomping his boots on the floor mat. "Nina, what's going on with you? Were you out in the cold too long?"

Probably. But that wasn't the problem. I was having a huge crisis with reality. If I couldn't find evidence that would tether me to the world I knew, then I truly would go crazy.

"I'm sorry guys. I had a weird epiphany while riding and would really like to see your wedding photos."

Papa and Grams exchanged a look that only a married couple who'd been together for years could understand. Grams released a sigh and went to the living room. From a drawer beneath the TV stand, she pulled an object out. She came back into the dining room, setting a maroon photo album in front of me.

I leaned over the book and flipped to the first page, finding a black and white photo of a young bride and groom, beaming at the camera. Grams was gorgeous in her lace dress, and Papa sure looked handsome in a suit. I flipped through multiple pages, and found myself stopping to stare at how happy my grandparents had been. They still were.

I approached the end of the album with no evidence of a date. The camera used at their wedding had been too old to put a date stamp in the corner of the photos. I reached the last page. Bingo! A wedding invitation. *You are cordially invited to a ceremony celebrating the love between Stephen Ulysses Pierson and Jaynie Elizabeth Walters on February 9, 1961.*

My shoulders relaxed, I sat back in my chair and released a loud sigh.

"Satisfied?" Grams asked.

"Yes." For now.

CHAPTER TWENTY-FOUR

THE NEXT MORNING, MY GRANDPARENTS FOLLOWED me with their eyes through every move I made in the kitchen. I'd really freaked them out. Couldn't blame them for being so vigilant. As of late, my behavior had become even more peculiar than usual. Papa knew a small part of the reason. Grams remained in the dark.

I joined them at the table with a cup of coffee and plate of eggs. I sniffed the contents of my mug, savoring the smell, but preparing my taste buds for a horrible taste. Running on a few hours of sleep wasn't going to get me through the day. My taste buds could make the sacrifice. I took a sip, forcing the liquid down.

Grams' brows rose. "All right, who are you and what have you done with my granddaughter?"

I laughed nervously. "What do you mean?"

"Nina Anderson is drinking coffee. Now I've seen everything," Papa said over his own mug.

I lifted one shoulder. "Thought I'd give it a try today. Perhaps I'll acquire a taste." I took another sip, nearly gagging on the bitterness.

"Shovel in those eggs, dear. Don't want to be late for church," Grams said, rising from the table.

I did as she said, barely chewing my breakfast. I forced down a couple more swallows of coffee as well. How long would it take for the caffeine to kick in?

After throwing on our coats and boots, we piled into Old Blue. It took Papa two tries before it would start. Most of the snow had melted, but the cold remained. Thankfully, I stayed warm and cozy squished between my grandparents.

As we rode into town, I couldn't help but be on the lookout for anything out of the ordinary. Despite being exhausted, my eyes were wide and my brain on high alert. Perhaps that was the result of the coffee. But more than likely I was hypersensitive and a smattering of adrenaline remained from yesterday.

Papa pulled into the parking lot of the quaint cobblestone church I'd grown accustomed to. While the congregation was small, the spirit and love of those who attended was larger than life. Since the incident with Jeremy, the people of the church had wrapped me in their loving embraces. Not once had I felt judged.

Papa turned off the truck and the three of us climbed out. I grabbed Grams' arm, helping her across the parking lot. "Be careful, Papa, there are some slick spots."

Papa held onto the side of the truck, joining Grams and me at the front of it. I grabbed Papa's arm as well, hoping to be a crutch should either of them start to go down. We carefully took the steps to the front door where pumpkins and wreaths made of leaves adorned the entryway. Inside the sanctuary, the scent of apple cider lingered. The smell eased the anxiety I still carried from yesterday.

The simple wooden pews and understated design of the church were homey and welcoming. Whenever I walked in I felt instantly comfortable. Amazing how stepping into a place of worship, no matter how extravagant or ordinary, could heal the heart.

As we walked through the sanctuary, Grams cheerfully shared the news of Papa's cancer with everybody we encountered. Papa smiled sheepishly and thanked them for their prayers. We weren't in the clear completely. There was always a chance that the cancer could come back. But I was incredibly grateful that God had healed Papa. The power of prayer was an amazing thing. Not long ago I'd pondered the point, but now I knew God worked in His own way and in His own timing.

At ten o'clock on the dot, the worship team found their spots on the stage, readying their instruments. Grams led the way to our usual spot—front and center. I spotted the Nelson family walking in, and instead of turning away like I usually did, I smiled and waved. Lulu bounced up and down as she waved vigorously in return. The little family found a pew toward the back and took their seats.

The worship leader stepped up to the microphone. "Good morning. Please stand with us as we worship our Lord," she said.

Worship had become my favorite thing about church. Each week I looked forward to hearing which songs the team had picked. Every song seemed to be chosen for me as they spoke directly to my heart. Even though I could hardly carry a tune, I found myself belting out the lyrics. Some people felt God the most while praying, others while reading from His word. It was while I sang that I truly felt God's presence.

As the worship team played their instruments, I didn't recognize the tune. The worship leader leaned into the microphone. "We have a new song for you all. It's one of my favorites by Bethel Music called No Longer Slaves. The lyrics are on the screen, so join in when you feel comfortable."

The words to the song spoke to me right away. Tears welled in my eyes, and I tried singing along but found myself choking up. The idea of not being a slave to fear because I'm a child of God was a concept I had never considered or even grasped. My fear of Jeremy had held me captive for too many years. I had allowed that fear to rule me because I wasn't trusting God to free me of it. I'd seen my life without God. And I didn't like it. Life was hard enough, but without God, it was impossible.

A tear rolled down my cheek, and I wiped it away. Grams grabbed my hand, giving it a gentle squeeze. Funny how the people we love the most know exactly the comfort we need at the right moment. Tears clouded my vision, and the lump in my throat prevented me from being able to sing the remainder of the songs.

The worship leader prayed that our hearts would be open to the pastor's words and then requested we greet the people around us. I dabbed at my eyes with a Kleenex before turning to my neighbors.

The older woman behind me held out her hand and said good morning. I shook her hand, greeting her in return with my best smile. My eyes grazed the sanctuary entrance. My smile and stomach dropped. A figure in all black with a hood shielding his face stood in the doorway. Was this the Rogue leader?

I sucked in my breath. He didn't stir as I gazed directly at him. All sound vanished from the room. Every other being in the sanctuary became faceless blurs.

"Miss? Miss?" The voice sounded hollow. Who was talking?

Somebody moved in my line of vision, blocking my view of the man at the back of the church. The surrounding noises returned. I blinked, and the face of the woman whose hand I still held came into focus.

Her brows rose. "Miss, are you okay?"

I released the woman's hand and craned my neck, looking past her. The man in black no longer stood in the doorway. I darted furtive glances around the sanctuary. No sign of him. Where did he go? What was he doing here? Was I in danger of another hallucination?

Grams grabbed my arm. I glanced down at her sitting in the pew. Apparently, the pastor had told the congregation to take their seats. I was the only one still standing. My cheeks flushed and I plopped down beside Grams.

She leaned in to me. "What's wrong?"

I shook my head hard.

"Are you feeling ill?" She put the back of her hand to my forehead. "You're so pale."

"I'm fine," I whispered. But I wasn't. I was far from fine. I thought I was safe from my demons while at church.

My knee bounced incessantly as the pastor began his message. What hallucination would the Rogue leader spring on me next?

As the sermon continued, my senses went on overload. Every cough made me twitch, and I turned my head to every movement caught in my peripheral vision. I closed my eyes, breathing in deeply. The stench of vinegar invaded my nose. My eyes sprang open.

They're here.

I clutched Grams' hand and leaned over her so Papa could hear me as well. "We have to get out of here."

Papa's brows pulled together. "Why? What's wrong?"

"You are feeling sick, aren't you?" Grams whispered.

If that was what would convince her to leave with me, then that's what I'd lead her to believe. "Yes. Very sick."

Papa squinted at me. My eyes widened as I tried to tell him without words what was really going on. He nodded, then grabbed Grams' arm. "Let's go with her, Jaynie. Maybe she needs fresh air."

"Good idea," Grams answered.

The three of us rose, awkwardly scooting past the others in our pew. I ignored the strange looks we received as we traveled down the aisle. The closer we got to the doorway, the stronger the vinegar smell became. We were almost to the double doors. But what about the others in the congregation? Would they be safe? I was about to stop my grandparents when a striking pain ricocheted off my skull. I let out a scream as I clutched my head.

Vaguely, I felt Grams and Papa grabbing me. I barely heard them asking me what was wrong. The agony in my head intensified, and I fell to my knees. My brain felt as though it were being split in two. I couldn't breathe, I couldn't think, all I could do was cry out in pain.

You're mine, Nina. A dark voice whispered across my mind

just before the pain ceased.

I continued to hold my head, a throbbing ache taking the former pain's place. Why was the Rogue leader targeting me? He was seeking me out specifically, yet I wasn't leaning towards evil. So why was he doing this?

Slowly, I opened my eyes. It took a moment for them to focus. My grandparents were kneeling in front of me, worry written across their faces.

Grams grabbed hold of my cheeks. "Nina, look at me." Tears welled in her eyes. "What's wrong?"

The stench of vinegar was still present. Everybody needed to get out of the church. "We need people to leave. Now."

Grams looked at me as though I'd gone insane. I looked to Papa. "Papa. Get people out of here."

He nodded and stood. "Ladies and gentleman, please don't panic, but it would be in everybody's best interest to leave immediately."

Grams stroked my cheek. "Darling, please tell me what's going on."

My chin quivered. "I can't, Grams."

A man from the congregation stood, his hands planted firmly on his hips. "What's the meaning of this, Stephen?"

A crowd gathered around me, staring at me with concerned looks. Surely they were judging me now. I'd interrupted the church service by screaming and falling to the floor like a mad woman.

The vinegar odor multiplied to the point I could almost taste it. My stomach twisted and I fought back the urge to dry heave. How many Rogues were here?

My eyes locked with a teenage girl who was standing with the crowd assembled around me. She didn't blink as she stared at me. Slowly, her pupils dilated. I swallowed hard and looked to the young man to her left. He too stared at me blankly. His pupils grew to the size of his irises.

I scrambled to my feet and faced the congregation. "Everybody get out now!"

The doors behind us slammed shut. I spun around. The guy and girl who I'd just noticed were guarding the door, along with another young couple.

"Nobody is leaving," the four of them said in unison.

CHAPTER TWENTY-FIVE

LIAM FOLLOWED VIOLET CLOSELY BEHIND AS she headed through the overgrown trees. Damian and Kimmie brought up the rear of their little army. What remained of the recent snow crunched beneath their feet.

They were about ten miles west of the clearing in an area Liam swore they had searched before. The land was starting to look the same. The four of them had combed every inch for miles over the past few days. Liam was starting to think that the Rogue passage wasn't anywhere near Despair. If it was, it was hidden incredibly well.

Violet suddenly stopped and tipped her head. While all Martyrs had an enhanced sense of hearing, hers was stronger than most. Liam cocked his head, but heard nothing out of the ordinary.

"What is it, Violet?" Kimmie whispered.

Violet pointed to Damian and indicated for him to go south, and Kimmie to turn east. Liam was assigned north, while she would go west.

Liam didn't like the idea of splitting up. But they could cover more ground that way. "Be careful," Liam mouthed to each of them.

With a slight nod, his team disappeared through the brush in their respective directions.

Liam ducked and twisted around thick branches, attempting to be as quiet as possible. His footfalls would be impossible for human ears to pick up on. Rogues, however, could hear them from a mile away.

The stench of vinegar hit him so abruptly that he nearly gagged. His eyes watered from the intensity. Liam glanced around, expecting a Rogue to be right next to him, but only the trees remained in sight.

Adrenaline pumped through his veins. He had to be close. Was his team okay? Had any of them come across anything? He wouldn't be able to call out to them, at least not without giving away their locations.

Liam looked over his shoulder. He should try to get to them. They were stronger in numbers. But this was the first Rogue clue he'd encountered since he started his search. If he left now, he may not be able to track down the area again. This was his only shot.

Nearly tiptoeing, he continued in the direction of the scent. A part of him knew he should turn back and find the others. But he couldn't bring himself to do so.

Five minutes passed. Then another. The smell of vinegar didn't get any stronger, but it wasn't fading either. Was it a trick? Perhaps he was getting too close to the passage and was being led away.

Liam stepped over a fallen tree trunk when a line of dense blue fog suddenly rolled across his feet, bringing with it an icy chill that caused even him to shiver. His heart hammered in his chest. He stepped back a few paces. The mist followed his trail and swirled around his ankles. He held his breath and stiffened as the mist snaked up his body. It stopped when it reached his face, coiled away and darted off, disappearing completely.

With a loud sigh, he relaxed his shoulders. That decided it, he needed to find his team. Liam spun around only to find Violet a few feet away.

"Did you see that?" He asked.

She nodded slightly.

"We're close. Have you seen the others?"

She shook her head.

Liam hooked his thumb over his shoulder. "I think we should go this way."

Violet pointed in the opposite direction.

"You sure?"

Without a word, Violet turned and began walking the other way.

On their previous searches, Violet had picked up on things he and the others hadn't been able to. He trusted her instincts.

Liam followed Violet as she wound her way around downed trees. He felt the hairs on the nape of his neck stand on end as they wove through the forest. Every noise had him on edge. With each glance over his shoulder, his eyes became wider.

The smell of vinegar became stronger with each step he took. Violet was right. They were headed in the right direction. What were they walking into? How many Rogues would be there?

The two of them wouldn't be able to take on many on their own. If they were coming up on the passage, they'd need to mark the location and go back to get the others.

Where were they anyway? He didn't think that the forest went this deep. Violet's speed suddenly increased.

"Violet!" he hissed. "Wait!"

But she kept walking. Liam realized they could be heading into a trap. The others wouldn't know where to find them. They had to turn around.

Liam came to a halt. "Violet, stop!"

She did as he said, turning briefly. A slow smile spread across her face. Violet rarely smiled. Something wasn't right.

She giggled. Liam's heart sank. Violet never laughed.

With every one of his senses on high alert, he backed away a couple steps.

Imposter Violet continued to smile. "You won't get to them in time."

Liam's eyes widened. He shouldn't give in to what this

illusion wanted. Interacting with it would only make it more real. But he had to know.

"Get to who?"

With a sinister sneer, her form began to fade as though she were a ghost.

Liam leapt forward, grabbing for her. His hand clutched only air and he was left alone in the woods, listening to her disembodied cackle.

CHAPTER TWENTY-SIX

MY HEART BEAT IN DOUBLE TIME. The foursome didn't appear to have any weapons. Were there other Rogues within the congregation, waiting to strike? Or perhaps the church was surrounded.

My eyes roamed the sanctuary, searching for emergency exits. Two doors sandwiched the stage, but both were guarded by people I assumed were taken over by Rogues. They held the same stance as the group shielding the main entrance.

Families of the congregation huddled together, their eyes wide with fear. Gasps and prayers rang out.

This is all my fault. Had I led the Rogues here? Were they coming after me because of what had happened with Carl?

Grams and Papa encircled me. Papa's eyes held panic. "What's happening, sweet pea?"

"I'm not quite sure."

Grams clutched her chest. "Who are those teenagers?"

"You haven't seen them in the church before?"

She shook her head. "I don't think so. I usually recognize everybody."

So they weren't part of the congregation. Had they been sitting within the pews this morning, and the Rogues chose the same time to take over their bodies for this cause? What was their cause?

The Rogues guarding the doors had yet to move. They simply stared down anybody who dared look them in the eye. Most people didn't for very long. Their dilated eyes left one's stomach very unsettled.

Commotion between a man and woman standing within the pews caught my eye. The woman held onto the arm of her husband, pulling at him. "No, please don't."

The man set his mouth in a straight line and ignored his wife's pleas as he tore away from her and headed for the group standing at the entrance.

I stepped forward. "Don't!" But I was too late. The moment he got within two feet of one of the Rogues, he was on the ground. The girl who'd pushed him had done so with such speed that I hadn't seen her do it. The man slid across the floor, slamming into a pew. His wife rushed to his side.

I looked to Grams. "Do you know of any other way out of here?"

She put her fingers to her lips and closed her eyes, then slowly shook her head. We were trapped.

Papa lifted his chin, sniffing the air. "What's that smell?"

"Vinegar," I said.

"No, not that." He inhaled deeper. "It smells like smoke."

My heart dropped into my stomach. I'd been so focused on the stench of vinegar I hadn't noticed. I took a whiff. Something was burning. The three of us glanced around the room, trying to find the source.

"Fire!" Somebody yelled.

We turned our heads toward the main entrance. Smoke billowed from beneath the door, snaking around the Rogues guarding it. Oh no. They were going to burn us alive.

Rage boiled behind my ears. I clenched my fists and stomped toward the Rogues.

"Nina, stop!" Papa called.

I ignored him and continued my trek. The four Rogues watched me, trying to intimidate me with their icy stares. I stopped directly in front of them. "Let me talk to your leader."

No response.

I gritted my teeth. "Let me talk to him. Now."

The four looked at each other before finally nodding. They stepped back, gesturing their hands toward the double doors.

That was it? It was as simple as that? It had to be a trick. But I was willing to risk whatever I needed to get these people out.

I took tentative steps toward the doors. I heard Grams and Papa screaming for me, but I couldn't allow them to hinder me from stopping this. Somehow, I knew I was the only one who could.

Cautiously, I placed my hands on the handles. They felt cool to the touch. It was now or never. *Lord, give me strength.* With a deep breath, I swung open the doors.

A blast of heat sucked the air from my lungs and knocked me to the floor. My eyes blurred, my throat constricted. I tried to cough, but I couldn't. Through tear-filled eyes I watched the fire roar from the foyer. The flames swayed, entrancing me with their dance. For a moment, I had the urge to reach out to the blaze and become a part of their tango.

"Nina!" Grams' voice called. Two sets of hands grabbed my arms, pulling me from the doorway. I could suddenly breathe as a coughing fit wracked my body.

The commotion around me happened in slow motion. The six rogues within the sanctuary ran for the double doors, disappearing into the fire of the foyer. The fire blazed with shades of blue. Hordes of people ran for the emergency exits, slamming their bodies against the doors as they desperately tried to get them open. The doors weren't budging.

Families wept and held onto each other. Others were on their knees, begging for mercy. A group of men grabbed for the double doors. Closing them wouldn't keep the fire from getting in. It would only delay the inevitable. Just before the doors shut, I caught a glimpse of the man in black. He stood among the flames, untouched. He pointed directly at me, then turned his finger as he beckoned me to join him.

I'm yours. The thought was suddenly projected into my mind, masquerading as my own. Or had I really thought it? Either way, yes. I was his.

I shook my head. No. I wasn't.

Grams' hands were suddenly on my cheeks. She turned me toward her, forcing me to look into her eyes. The look of terror on her face made me want to weep.

Papa was busy patting my arms, my legs, my torso. "I don't think she's been burned, Jaynie."

"How is that possible? The flames swarmed her body."

They had? And I wasn't burned?

My grandparents stared at me in disbelief. "Nina, honey, can you talk?" Grams asked.

Could I? My throat felt scratchy but unharmed. "Yes," I managed to rasp.

My eyes suddenly landed on a family hunkered down in the pew beside us. The Nelsons. Mr. Nelson clutched his wife in one arm and Lulu in the other. Kevin Jr. clung to his mother. Lulu's eyes met mine. The fear on her face told me she knew she was going to die. A sob caught in my throat.

She was in danger yet again because of me. Forty or so lives would be lost because of me. I had to do something. There had to be a way to get out. Whatever it was, we had to find it fast. The smoke had thickened and the sound of coughing intensified. The doors were out, but what about the windows?

I skimmed the room. The eight stained-glass windows were big enough to fit people through, but they were so high. We'd need a twelve-foot ladder, and I doubted we could find one within the sanctuary.

First thing, we needed to seal off the doors as much as possible. I grabbed Grams' arm. "Listen to me, Grams. You need to find cloth to block the smoke from coming in through the doors."

She shook her head. "I can't. I can't."

I clutched her shoulders. "Yes, you can. Find some people to help you. You can do this." I gave her a kiss on the forehead. She reached for me, locking me in a tight embrace. Once I was released, she did the same to Papa.

"Be careful," Papa whispered to her.

Grams stood on shaky knees and hustled down the aisle toward the stage. Papa watched her with worry etched on his brow.

I grabbed his hand. "She'll be okay, Papa. We need to find something to get us up to the windows."

Papa looked up, scanning the windows. "They're so high."

I squeezed his fingers. "We'll make a human chain if we have to. Everybody is getting out of here alive."

He set his mouth in a taut line and gave a quick nod.

Coming to my feet, I pulled Papa up with me and wrapped him in a hug. "I love you, Papa." It wasn't a goodbye. I only wanted him to know. Just in case.

"I love you too, sweet pea."

I leaned away. "Let's go."

Papa took off down the aisle, stopping to talk with groups huddled together. I rushed to the Nelsons, crouching down in front of them. "You all are going to get out of here. Just hold tight. Stay low."

"I called 911," Mr. Nelson said. "The fire department is on their way."

My heart sank. The church was on the outskirts of town. The fire station was at least fifteen minutes away. By the time rescuers would reach us, the church and everybody within it would be reduced to ash.

Oh, Liam, I need you!

I swallowed hard and rose, running down the aisle to where Papa explained to the pastor what we planned to do.

Grams and a few other women had found tablecloths and were stuffing them beneath the doors. Already, the smoky air had lightened, but it would only be a temporary fix. How much time did we have before the fire consumed the entire building?

Panic rose. Screams, cries, and prayers become louder. We needed to get people calmed down. I leapt onto the stage, grabbing a microphone and putting it to my lips. "Listen up!"

The noise level lowered, and it was then that we could hear the roaring of the fire. Wood popped and cracked. We were running out of time.

"We're working to figure out a way to get out, but we need everybody to remain calm."

Some nodded. Others continued to cry silently. When death loomed, staying calm was a nearly impossible task, but it was our only chance at survival.

I hopped down from the stage and joined Papa and Pastor Johnson.

Pastor Johnson looked at me. "If we're going to get through the windows, the nearest ladder is in a closet in the foyer."

Well that was out of the question. What other option was there though? I studied the space between the floor and one of the windows. It would take a couple of tall men standing on shoulders to reach the window sill. What could we stack? Chairs? Pews?

I glanced around the room, searching for the tallest item in the room. But wait, how would people get down on the other side? Jump? That wasn't going to work. There were too many children and elderly within the congregation.

"Pastor, I need you to think really hard. Is there any other way out?"

He ran his hand over his chin. "There's a crawl space beneath the church, but I've never been in it. I don't know if there's a way outside."

It was something at least and could be our only hope. We had to try. "How do you get to it?"

"It's behind the stage." He hopped onto the platform. Papa

and I followed.

An archway at the back of the stage led to a storage area. Christmas costumes and other decorations took up the majority of the space. Pastor Johnson rolled a clothing rack away from the wall where a latch in the floor was hidden.

He unhooked the latch and lifted the wooden door. The hole was just big enough to fit one person, and the drop was only a few feet down to a dirt floor. Papa knelt, starting to climb in.

I grabbed his shoulder. "What are you doing?"

"Going to check it out."

I shook my head. "No. I'm doing it."

I crawled down into the pit, laying on my belly. The musty smell and spider webs wouldn't keep me from finding an exit. The darkness however would make it hard.

"Pastor, does your phone have a flashlight?"

A smart phone with a white light gleaming from a corner dropped beside me. I picked it up and shined the light to my left toward the front of the church where the fire still blazed. It wouldn't be safe to go that way. I directed the light in front of me. Not far ahead was a dead end. My feet hit the cinder block wall behind me as well. Going to the right was my only choice.

I used my elbows and knees to turn and slide on my stomach, propelling myself around the small space. I prayed for a light to shine in from a hole or crack in the foundation, but the farther I crawled, the less hope I had.

I was about to turn back when a mouse ran in front of me. Ordinarily I would have screamed in terror, but a tiny mouse was the least of my worries. Hold on. How did a mouse get in here?

I shined the light on it. The creature ran and stopped multiple times as I followed along to the cinder block wall. Far in the corner, it squeezed through a little hole in the concrete. A small sliver of light streamed in. I poked my finger through the hole, then pushed on the cinder block. It scraped against the block beside it. It was loose! If I could find something to loosen it

146

further, perhaps I could knock it out. But the hole still wouldn't be big enough for a person to fit through. Were any of the others wobbly? I pushed on the block above. It gave as well.

I crawled back to the hatch opening as fast as I could. Papa and Pastor Johnson peered down at me with eager expressions.

"There are a couple cinder blocks loose. I need something to knock them out with."

Pastor disappeared from my view. He returned a moment later with a metal bar that I assumed was from the clothing rack. "Will this work?"

"I'll give it a try." I grabbed it from him and held it under my arm as I scooted back to the corner.

With the position I was in, would I be able to put enough force behind each blow? Still on my belly, I choked up on the bar with both hands, pulled it back and slammed it into the top cinder block. It moved. Barely. I readied myself yet again and shoved the bar into it. I continued this until sweat dripped from my brow and my hands became blistered.

A scream suddenly echoed above me.

"Papa! What's going on?"

"I'll check it out," he called down into the crawl space.

This tactic was taking too long. The cinder block had only moved a few inches within the few minutes I'd been pummeling it.

"Sweet pea," Papa's voice shook. "The fire has gone through the door. We don't have much time."

Please, God, I need your help.

I flipped onto my back and twisted around, planting my feet on the cinder blocks. Adrenaline shot through my body as I gritted my teeth and pushed on the cement with my feet. I drew my knees back and smashed my feet over and over. My thighs burned. My jaw ached. But I continued until both cinder blocks gave and fell away from the rest of the wall.

I scrambled to my stomach again, moving toward the new

hole I had created. Sunlight poured in like a beacon of hope. The space was still rather small. Would everybody be able to fit?

"Sweet pea? How's it coming?" Papa called.

"We're good! Start rounding everybody up."

I crept back through to the entrance of the hatch, poking my head out. A crowd had formed inside the storage room.

"We'll send the children down first," Pastor said.

Parents gave their children hugs and kisses while the children clung to them. Moms and dads told their children that they'd see them soon, while their eyes said they weren't certain they would. Half-a-dozen children ranging from two to ten gathered around me. Lulu and Kevin Jr. were among them, their tear-stricken faces looking to me for comfort.

I had to explain fast, but tried to remain calm for the kids' sakes. "It's kind of dirty down here, but you'll have to get down on your belly and crawl."

"Kind of like in the army?" One of the older boys asked.

I smiled despite the pain in my heart. "Yes, exactly. I'll lead the way, so you stay as close as you can to the person in front of you. When you get outside, find a tree far away from the church. That's where your parents will meet you."

I gave one last look to the parents staring at me as they wiped their eyes. They entrusted me to get their children to safety. That's exactly what I was going to do.

"Papa, will you and Pastor lower the kids down?"

Papa nodded.

"All right, let's go." I got on my stomach once again and began crawling. Halfway to our destination I stopped and looked back. "Everybody okay?"

Voices of varying pitches answered yes, and I continued on our way. When I reached the hole I'd created, I motioned for the child behind me to move up beside me. The oldest boy scooted along, inching his way to the hole. His body fit through the narrow space easily, but there were some people waiting above us that were three times his size.

The next three children fit through even easier as they were smaller than the first boy. The two kids remaining were Lulu and Kevin Jr.

Lulu grabbed my arm. "I can't leave my mommy and daddy," she squeaked.

I placed my hand on top of hers. "They'll be okay, Lulu. I promise I'll get them out."

She reached around my back, giving me an awkward hug in the tight space.

I choked on a sob threatening to make an escape. I swallowed it down. If I let it out, I'd never stop crying. And these people needed me to have a level head. "You need to go, sweetie."

Lulu released me and shimmied through the hole. Kevin Jr. whimpered as he moved past me. He was small enough he could be on his hands and knees. Lulu was on the other side of the hole, reaching for his hands. She grabbed his wrists and pulled him out.

I breathed a sigh of relief that the kids were safe. But I still had a lot of work to do. A moment later, a hand grabbed my ankle. I glanced back to find Ruthie.

"Did they get out okay?" she asked.

"Yes, they're fine."

Ruthie smiled slightly, then moved toward the hole. Her shoulders fit through fine, but she was petite. Her husband was thin, but had broader shoulders. He had to squeeze through at a weird angle, but he made it. Once outside, he gritted his teeth and pulled at one of the cinder blocks to widen the hole. It gave way and he flew backwards.

"Thank you," I said. "That should be good enough. Go join your children."

Ruthie helped Kevin Sr. to his feet. The two shot me looks of desperation as they took off for their kids.

A chain of people continued through the crawl space. When the floorboards began to creak and smoke drifted down into the space, it was then that I started to panic. Grams and Papa had yet to come down.

I turned around, heading back for the hatch. Others continued to file through.

"Papa! Grams!" I called when I reached the crawlspace entrance.

Coughs sounded above me. "We're coming, dear," Grams' hoarse voice replied.

This was taking too long. "How many more people do we have?" I asked.

"Only a few," Papa answered.

My grandparents were going to be the last ones. By their own choosing. Why couldn't they be selfish for once?

"Pastor, you're next," Papa said.

"No, no. You and Jaynie first."

The building shuddered so violently that I felt it in the ground.

"There's no time to argue," I said. "All of you get down here now!"

Pastor Johnson crawled down. He grabbed my hand. "Thank you so much, Nina."

Snaps and groans vibrated through the building. "Go, Pastor."

He scooted on his belly toward the hole. Grams came down next.

"Grams, you need to move as fast as you can."

"What about you?"

"I'll be right there. I'm going to make sure Papa gets down okay."

Grams kissed me on the cheek and slid away. Papa hopped in, coming to his stomach right away. "You first, sweet pea."

I shook my head. "I'm right behind you."

He was about to argue with me, until a crash sounded above us. My eyes widened. "Go, Papa! Now!"

Papa used all his power to scoot along the ground. I followed behind him, the crashes becoming louder above and behind us. The church was collapsing. We weren't going to make it. I glanced back, the fire moved toward us, absorbing everything it touched. Smoke surrounded us, making it impossible to do anything but focus on trying to get air into my lungs.

My eyes watered profusely. Was Papa through the hole yet? I continued to move forward, but doing so was becoming more difficult.

"Nina!" His muted voice called. I could see sunlight. I was almost there. I reached my hands toward the hole. Papa's fingers grazed mine.

I couldn't move any further. Why couldn't I move? Coughing racked my body and I desperately sucked in air. My eyes were becoming heavy. All I wanted to do was sleep.

"It's coming down!" Somebody yelled. "Get her out of there!"

Without warning, something heavy crashed down onto my back. I screamed out in agony. The pain. It was too much. Tears leaked out of the corners of my eyes. Whatever was on top of me was crushing me. And it was hot. So very hot.

"Nina!" Grams cried.

I wasn't going to make it out. *Lord, I'm ready.*

More debris and rubble fell around me. The last thing I heard was my grandparents' cries.

CHAPTER TWENTY-SEVEN

LIAM GLANCED AROUND FRANTICALLY. LAUGHS OF varying pitches echoed throughout the forest. The smell of vinegar continued to permeate the air. How many Rogues were out there? He couldn't believe he'd fallen for a hallucination. He thought he'd be able to know the difference between what was real and what wasn't.

Liam took off in the direction he thought he'd come from, but he didn't get very far before he skidded to a stop. He gasped at the sight of a wide lake suddenly in front of him. What if he couldn't get out of this illusion? He didn't believe he was close to the passage. That couldn't be why he was being tricked. What was the leader trying to keep him away from? His stomach dropped. Was he still going after Nina?

With renewed purpose to get out, Liam toed the water carefully. It felt as real as the panic beginning to rise in his chest. The lake seemed to go on for miles. There was no way he'd be able to swim the length without a horrible fate befalling him.

He ran in the other direction, leaping over stumps. Monstrous trees were placed in his path like magic. He was fast enough to maneuver around before smashing into them. Just when he thought he was reaching the end of the forest, the ground began to rumble. He stopped and watched hundreds of birds fly out of the trees. A loud pop sounded below him. He glanced between his feet. The soil was sinking like quick sand.

With a gasp, Liam stepped back. "No!" He screamed as his feet sunk into the ground. The earth tried to swallow him whole as the dirt reached his knees. He struggled and wriggled until he was able to free himself. With a bound, he made it off the trail and into the grass. He leaned against a tree, catching his breath.

He was never going to get out of the illusion. Where was his team? He cupped his hands around his mouth. "Kimmie! Damian! Violet!"

All at once, he heard their voices scream his name from every direction. Was it really them? Or was it all a ruse?

"Liam!" Nina's voice called amongst the others.

His heart leapt and he spun around, trying to single out Nina's voice. It wasn't her. It couldn't be. None of this was real.

Liam closed his eyes and took a deep breath as he tried to calm himself.

Liam! Nina's voice faintly whispered across his mind. For a brief moment, he felt her fear and panic.

His eyes sprang open. She was in trouble.

The false voices of his team continued to echo around him, trying to distract him from hearing Nina's thoughts. Nothing was going to keep him from her.

Lord, help me get out of here.

Liam pinched his eyes shut and clamped his hands over his ears. "This isn't real! Show me what is!"

Abruptly, all noise ceased. Liam slowly opened his eyes and pulled his hands from his ears. Everything was still. And the smell of vinegar was no longer present. He spun around, looking at every tree and landmark carefully. It all seemed real.

Screams suddenly pierced the air. Liam jerked his head in the direction they'd come from. Grey smoke twisted into the sky.

With speed only gifted to a Martyr, he raced toward the smoke and was able to make his way out of the forest. *Lord, please let Nina be okay,* he prayed over and over.

His heart leapt when he arrived on the scene. Families were gathered a fair distance from the church that was ablaze and crumbling fast. He searched for Nina among the crowd, but he didn't spot her.

It was then that he saw her grandparents on their hands and knees directly next to the fiery structure, reaching through an opening in the concrete wall. "Nina!" they cried.

Oh, no. She was still inside. A Martyr wasn't supposed to do anything to bring attention to themselves. However, in that moment, he didn't care. He darted across the field, stooping beside Nina's grandparents.

"Where is she?" he asked.

Her grandmother's tears stopped momentarily to look at him with confusion. "Liam?"

"She's in the crawl space." Her grandfather said. "Just beyond that hole. The rubble has fallen and we can't—"

Liam didn't need to hear anything more. Using his unearthly strength, he punched through the concrete stones. The pain didn't register in his mind, even as his fist came away bloodied after each blow. When he'd made an opening large enough to pass through, he wasted no time crawling in.

Burning beams and other rubble littered the tight space. Smoke clouded his vision and breathing didn't come easily.

"Nina!" he said through a cough.

No response.

His stomach tightened, and his heart hammered. Where was she? He chucked pieces of wood that no ordinary man would have been able to lift. A piece of flooring burned directly in front of him. He lifted it only to hear a slight gasp come from underneath.

Nina.

He flung the panel away, finding Nina's still form. He grabbed hold of her, pulling her to him and shielding her with his body. He didn't have time to check if she was still breathing. Tucking her in his arms the way a child would a doll, he slid out through the hole. He came to his feet immediately, cradling his love.

"Oh, thank God," her grandmother wept.

They weren't in the clear yet. Her grandparents followed after him. As soon as he was a safe distance from the church, he lay Nina down in the soggy grass.

Her clothing was dirty and torn. Ash covered the majority of her face and the ends of her hair were singed. Miraculously, she didn't appear to be burned. Liam put his fingers to her neck, checking for a pulse. She had one, but she wasn't breathing. He pinched her nose and put his mouth to hers, releasing a long string of air. Her chest rose as Liam's breath filled her lungs. Would simple CPR do it, or would he need to use another method? He pulled away, waiting for a sign of consciousness. Her mouth fell slack.

"Come on, Nina," he whispered. He put his mouth on hers once again, breathing into her even longer. He pulled away, willing her to cough, open her eyes, anything to show life.

Nothing.

Her grandfather remained silent, while her grandmother cried hysterically. Liam looked at her papa. His eyes begged him to do what he'd witnessed that night at the Nelsons'.

Liam nodded. He closed his eyes and found that inner part of him that allowed him the ability to heal. Warmth emanated from his core and shot through his veins. He leaned down, about to give Nina the kiss of life when her back arched and she sucked in air.

IT HURT. MY GOODNESS it hurt. Not only did my lungs ache to the point I thought they were on fire, but a skull cracking headache set in immediately. I opened my eyes, but doing so caused a striking pain to shoot through my brain. I snapped my eyes shut and released a moan as I clutched my head.

"Thank God," Papa said a little too loudly. His voice vibrated through my mind.

"Nina, honey, where do you hurt?" Grams asked.

Everywhere. I hurt everywhere. My back ached as though an elephant had sat on it. And what was that smell? Burnt hair? I tried to speak, but my throat stung too badly.

"Thank you so much, Liam," Grams said. "How did you get through the wall?"

Liam was here? I forced my eyes open. His beautiful face stared down at me. The concern etched in his brow made me want to weep. I wanted nothing more than to reach up and stroke his cheek. But I couldn't. For one, I didn't think I had enough strength to do something so simple. And secondly, he was no longer mine to touch affectionately.

Liam drew in a deep breath and pulled his gaze from me to look at Grams. "It must have been an adrenaline rush."

Did she buy it? Her brows wrinkled further. "What are you even doing here?"

"I'm visiting my grandparents for a few days."

She nodded. "Aw, yes. The Thiessens, right?"

That wasn't the name I'd given her this summer. I couldn't remember what I told her.

No, Liam! That's not it!

"Correct," Liam answered.

I closed my eyes. Oh no. We were caught in a lie.

Grams squinted. "Hmm."

Sirens echoed in the distance. The high-pitched alarms made me groan and grit my teeth. Did they have to be so loud? The closer they came, the harder it was to concentrate on anything but the ear-splitting noise.

I had a sudden urge to sit up. I lifted my neck, but a strong hand rested on my forehead, preventing me from moving. "It's best if you remain still," Liam said. "An ambulance is here. They're going to take good care of you."

He moved his hand to my cheek, stroking it with his

156

knuckles. I closed my eyes, soaking in the fleeting moment. When would he be able to touch me again? Would there be a next time?

I pointed to my temple, hoping he'd understand I wanted him to listen to my thoughts.

Rogues did this.

Liam frowned. "I know."

The leader was here.

His brows pulled together.

A pair of EMTs were at my side then. Liam moved aside, and my cheek ached to have him touch me again. In a blur, the EMTS checked my vitals and placed an oxygen mask over my mouth as they asked my grandparents my name and details about what had happened.

A male EMT hovered over me. "Nina, can you tell me if anything hurts?"

"My back," I mumbled through the mask.

"Do you have any numbness in your extremities?"

I shook my head.

"Can you wiggle your fingers and toes for me?"

I did as he said.

"We're going to put you onto the gurney now. We'll be as gentle as possible." He counted to three and the pair lifted me into the air. Pain shot through my spine, but diminished as soon as I was on the gurney.

Grams and Papa each held one of my hands as the EMTs wheeled me toward the ambulance. "Everything will be okay, sweetheart. Papa and I will meet you at the hospital."

"Liam?" I managed to screech.

Papa glanced over his shoulder. "He's already gone."

Figured. I shouldn't have been upset, but I was. I knew he needed to investigate the fire. But I wanted him to be with me.

The EMTs lifted me and the gurney into the ambulance. I looked to my grandparents who stood on the outside. Tears streamed down Grams' cheeks as Papa gripped her shoulders.

Behind them, firemen sprayed water onto what remained of the church.

Right before the ambulance doors closed, my eyes found Liam standing too close for comfort near the burning building. Conflicting emotions passed over his face, battling for dominance. Rage won and his eyes narrowed. Somehow I knew that this meant war with the Rogues.

CHAPTER TWENTY-EIGHT

THE AMBULANCE RIDE TO THE HOSPITAL was a long one. Every minor bump in the road jostled me enough to make my back twinge and my head pound. The EMTs took my vitals every five minutes and asked me the same questions over and over. I'd already told them my full name, where I'd been born, and my birthdate three times. Were they taking down notes or simply making sure I remained coherent?

The long ride allowed me time to think. Normally, I would avoid thoughts of the Rogues, but the thinking kept my mind off the pain in my body. It still didn't make sense why the Rogue leader was after me. Had I seen too much? Did he know that Liam and I still had feelings for each other? Did he know that by setting the church on fire, Liam would come to my rescue?

Oh, no! Was it a trap? Could Liam be in danger right at that moment? A gang of Rogues could be waiting to strike.

I pulled the oxygen mask from my mouth. "I have to go back," I said, trying to lift off the gurney.

The female EMT placed her hand on my shoulder and forced the mask back on my face. "Lay back down, miss."

My eyes widened. "But I have to get back to him! He could be in danger!"

The EMT ignored me as she took my vitals yet again. I couldn't get to Liam. Where was he at that moment? Was he safe? Were the other Martyrs with him? Could they protect themselves? So many questions bombarded my mind, causing my headache to deepen.

Please protect him, God.

We finally arrived at the hospital. The EMT duo pulled me and the gurney out of the ambulance, and wheeled me through the emergency room doors of the Beloit hospital. When would my grandparents arrive? There was no way Old Blue could travel as fast as the ambulance.

I was wheeled into a room where the lights were far too bright. In the blink of an eye, I was lifted onto a hospital bed and told to remain flat on my back. Nurses began poking and prodding me, asking me all the same questions the EMTs had. A blood pressure cuff was wrapped around my left bicep, and an IV stabbed into my right arm. The nurse behind it drew my blood, then hung a bag from the IV pole and pressed multiple buttons on the machine.

Despite all the distress my body was going through, I couldn't help but be amazed by the performance of the medical personnel. It was like a dance. Each person had their special move and executed it to perfection.

A male doctor joined the crew, glancing at my chart. He looked me in the eye. "I'm Dr. Black. How are you feeling, Nina?"

I raised my brows. *You're kidding me.* "Could be worse," I mumbled.

The nurses seemed to be done with their part of the performance and Dr. Black took over. He turned my wrist over and stared at his watch as he took my pulse. He then placed the ends of his stethoscope in his ears and placed the cold end on my chest beneath my shirt.

"Heartbeat is strong. Albeit a little fast."

"Well, I did just escape a burning building," I said without humor.

He chuckled. "I understand a beam fell on your back. I'd like to send you in for an x-ray immediately." He jotted something down on my chart and motioned for a nurse who stood off to the side.

As the nurse wheeled me to my x-ray, I couldn't help but worry what they would find. What if something was broken? We arrived inside a small room that consisted of a machine that looked like equipment out of a sci-fi movie. A couple of other nurses were suddenly by my side, and the group lifted me from the bed to the x-ray table. The x-ray technician told me to be as still as possible, and ten minutes later all the necessary pictures had been taken.

Dr. Black was in my ER room when I returned, shuffling through my x-rays. "You are one lucky girl, Nina Anderson."

Grams and Papa walked into the room. "Not lucky, blessed," Grams said.

The doctor nodded at my grandparents then returned his attention to me. "It appears that your spine is only bruised. Nothing a little rest and pain relievers can't fix."

Well that was a relief.

"Your lungs looked healthy in the x-rays, but I need you to lean forward so I can listen to them." I winced as Dr. Black helped me into a seated position. He placed the stethoscope between my shoulder blades and told me to take a deep breath. I did as he said until my eyes blurred and my head felt as though it were made of lead.

Dr. Black pulled the ends of the stethoscope from his ears. "Are you having any dizziness, nausea, or headaches?"

"I have a splitting headache. And I recently started feeling dizzy."

Dr. Black helped me to lay back down. "Your lungs sound fine, but you could have carbon monoxide poisoning. We'll get the blood test soon to confirm."

"What do you do for that?" Papa asked.

"High-dose oxygen. We'll keep the mask on throughout the day. I'd like to keep you overnight to be safe." He lifted a mask from a cart beside him and fitted it over my face then patted my shoulder. "I'll return to check on you in a bit."

"Thank you, doctor."

"You bet." He gave me a sweet smile and swiped the blue curtain closed to give us privacy.

My grandparents stared at me, tears welling in their eyes. The dam was about to break for both of them. They didn't have to be strong for me.

I held out my arms. Papa came to one side, Grams the other, and they buried their faces in my chest as they wept. Grams' comforting smell of lemons drifted up my nose. I wrapped my arms around them. Tears leaked out of my eyes.

"Dear heavenly father," Papa said. He swallowed a few times before continuing. "Thank you so much for having your hand on Nina and that she is okay. Thank you for all the medical personnel taking care of our girl."

If it hadn't been for Liam, would I have died beneath the burning debris? The commotion of my examination had made me forget Liam for a moment. The worry set in again. He had to be okay, right? He knew how to take care of himself. Still, the not knowing almost killed me.

Papa cleared his throat as he fought off a sob. "Continue to look after Nina and help her to make a speedy recovery. In your son's name, amen."

"Amen," Grams and I said together.

My grandparents leaned away, wiping at their faces. I lifted my oxygen mask slightly to wipe at mine.

"How's my hair look?" I asked.

Grams stroked my hair from my forehead. "You may need a bit of a haircut."

I shrugged. "I was probably due for one anyway." A nurse came in then, checking my IV bag and pressing buttons on the machine.

"What is that?" Papa asked.

"Fluids to keep her hydrated and a bit of pain medication." She looked to me. "Your blood results came back, and you do have carbon monoxide poisoning. I'm sure the oxygen mask is uncomfortable, but it needs to stay on for the duration of your time here."

I nodded. "It's fine."

"I'll be back in a minute to get you cleaned up and help you change into a gown." She left and the room fell silent.

My grandparents could only stare at me. My goodnesss, I'd put them through so much in the last few months. Weren't they sick of it?

"I'm sorry," I whispered.

"For what, dear?"

For so much. So many people, including my grandparents almost died today. And their church was no longer there. Their safe haven and place of worship had ceased to exist.

It was too much. I couldn't take it anymore. Tears sprang from my eyes, and I flung my arms across my forehead. Sobs shook my body, causing the pain in my back to grow exponentially, but I couldn't stop weeping.

Two sets of hands stroked my arms. "Nina, it's okay," Papa said.

"It's all my fault," I muttered.

"Nonsense," Grams said. "You didn't set the fire."

No, but I might as well have. I never realized until that moment how every event causes ripples throughout one's own and others' lives. If I wouldn't have started dating Jeremy, I never would have been abused and he never would've tried to kill me. Then I wouldn't have met Liam, the Rogues wouldn't have a need for me, and the church wouldn't have been set on fire. It was all connected, and I was the common denominator.

My grandparents continued to comfort me until I ended up with hiccups. I waited for peace to settle over me, but it didn't come. A feeling of hopelessness swarmed me instead. Was any of this going to end? What if Liam and the Martyrs couldn't get rid of the Rogues? Even if they did, other passages existed in the world. As long as the Rogues were around, people would continue to commit evil acts.

"Nina," a soft male voice filled the room.

My tears stopped abruptly, and I tore my arm away from my eyes to find that Liam had joined us. Oh, thank God he was okay.

Grams went to Liam, wrapping her arms around his waist. "Thank you so much, Liam."

He tentatively wrapped one arm around her back and gave her a hug. After a moment, she pulled away and Papa went to him. He held out his hand, giving Liam's a firm shake. "You've saved her yet again."

Grams shot Papa a confused look. "Again? What do you mean?"

Papa grabbed Grams' arm. "Let's give them some time alone."

My grandparents left the room, but Liam's presence made the space feel every bit as crowded. I wanted to rip off the mask, leap into his arms and kiss away my feelings. Instead, I remained in the bed, staring at him and waiting for him to speak.

He rubbed at the back of his neck. "How are you feeling?"

I lifted one shoulder as I removed my oxygen mask temporarily. "Drowsy and achy. But I've had worse."

Liam winced.

"Were you hurt?" I asked.

"Don't worry about me."

"But I do. All the time. I can't help it."

The left corner of his mouth lifted. "I'm unharmed."

"Should you be here?"

He shrugged. "Probably not. But I had to see you and make sure you were okay."

"Physically, I'll be fine. Emotionally, I'm a wreck."

Liam shoved his hands in his jean pockets and stared down at the floor. The action made him seem so human. "I'm sorry. For causing you so much pain. If I'd never gotten involved with you then—"

"Stop it." A single tear rolled down my cheek. "I will never regret being with you. My only regret will be the events that led to you being necessary in my life. And what my involvement with you has done to my family and others in the community."

Liam nodded.

I closed my eyes. I couldn't believe what I was about to say. The band aid over my already broken heart was about to be ripped off. I swallowed hard and opened my eyes. "When you find the Rogue passage and destroy it, I want you to go back home and never visit me again."

Liam's head shot up, and his eyes met mine. He took a step forward. "Nina, don't do this."

I held up a hand, staying him. When he'd been the one to end things, our future had been up in the air. Neither of us had voiced our questions, but I think we both knew that once it was all over, we would find our way back to each other. But I realized now that couldn't happen.

"As long as we're together, won't the Rogues continue to try to get to you through me? That would be their ultimate prize, right? To win the soul of a Martyr?"

Liam nodded slowly.

"I don't care so much about the risk I put myself in, but I do care how it affects my family. I can't continue to put them in danger."

"Nina . . ."

"And once your mission is complete, we'll have to return to our two-hour a day relationship." A lump formed in my throat. "I want marriage, children, a normal life with you. But we'll never have that."

Liam closed his eyes and pinched the bridge of his nose. He took a deep breath and exhaled slowly. He dropped his hand and looked at me, tears filling his eyes. "This is it then."

I held my own tears at bay. "Yes."

"I love you, Nina. I always will."

I closed my eyes to keep from crying. "I'll always love you."

When I opened my eyes, he was gone. I sobbed until I couldn't breathe.

CHAPTER TWENTY-NINE

LOVE WAS THE PRIMARY EMOTION LIAM was created with. All other human emotions were inactive in a Martyr until they experienced something earthly that called forth a specific feeling. His first encounter with Nina, he'd been frightened because he'd just been placed and hadn't expected to find her there at the pond. His fear had turned to anger because of his confusion. That was his first taste of anger. He'd felt twinges of it when Nina would tell stories of her past with Jeremy. It had boiled within him that night at the Nelsons' and again when Carl attacked Nina.

He never realized the difference between rage and anger until he pulled Nina from the burning church. As he walked out of the hospital, that same rage burned behind his ears. It was because of the Rogues that evil existed. It was because of the Rogues that innocent people were wronged and suffered. And now it was because of the Rogues that he couldn't be with the woman he loved. He would do whatever it took to take them down and free Nina of this burden.

I DIDN'T EVEN TRY to hide my tears when my grandparents walked back into the room. They both shot me a sympathetic smile. I didn't want their pity. I didn't deserve it. I brought all of this on myself.

Grams sighed. "Nina, I have to ask about Liam. You told me his grandparents were the Smiths, but when I asked him today he told me a different name. He doesn't really have family around here, does he?"

I wiped my eyes and looked to Papa.

"I think we need to tell her, sweet pea."

I nodded and returned my attention to Grams. "Liam is . . . not of this world."

Grams' brows rose. "Excuse me?"

"He has supernatural abilities."

She shook her head. "I'm sorry, what?"

"Jaynie, what she says is true. I've seen what he can do. You saw it today when he busted through the cement."

She closed her eyes and held out her palm. "Wait a minute." She opened her eyes. "You're telling me he has super powers?"

A smile tried to sneak onto my face. "He calls them gifts."

"From whom? God? Is he an angel?"

"There are many things I still don't know about him. He can't tell me where he's from or how he obtained his gifts. And he isn't an angel."

"What is he then?"

I hadn't even told Papa this. "He's a Martyr. He was sent as my protector. He was the one who saved me that day at the Nelsons'."

Grams' mouth dropped open. "I need to sit down."

Papa went to her side, guiding her into a chair. Leaning forward, she rested her head in her hands and took a deep breath. She was silent for some time. What was she thinking? Did she believe us?

"Grams?"

She reclined back in the chair, looking from me to Papa. "Why didn't you two tell me before?"

I shrugged. "We didn't know how you'd react."

I still wasn't sure how she was reacting. Was she scared, skeptical, awed?

"I'm sorry, Jaynie," Papa said. "It wasn't my secret to tell."

She puffed up her cheeks and blew the air out slowly between her pursed lips. "I understand." She mashed her lips together, staring off into space.

Was she processing the news? Or piling up a list of questions? She'd always been so inquisitive. Must be where I got it from. If I were in her shoes, I'd be digging for as much information as I could.

"What are you thinking, Grams?" She turned to me, her eyes watering. "I'm thinking that I'm so glad Liam was there that night at the Nelsons' and today, otherwise you wouldn't be here talking to me."

I released a sigh. A weight lifted off my shoulders. Now the two people I loved most in the world knew my secret. Or at least part of it.

"Have your nightly rides been to see him?"

I nodded. "But that won't be happening anymore."

Grams cocked her head to the side. "Why not?"

I ran my hand over my face. "Because I ended things with him."

My grandparents' faces dropped into a frown.

"It's okay. I'm okay. Things are too complicated."

I had the strong urge to tell them all about the Rogues and who started the fire, but I couldn't. They didn't need to worry about one more thing. Their world had been rocked enough.

The nurse returned, bringing with her a small tub of water and a sponge. "Would you prefer I clean you up or would you like to do it yourself?" she asked.

I looked to Grams. "Would you mind helping me?"

She nodded. "Of course, dear." She rose from her chair and took the sponge from the nurse.

The nurse opened a drawer beneath the hospital bed and pulled out a gown, laying it at the foot of the bed. "Press the nurse button on the rail if you need anything." She gave me a soft smile and left the room.

"I'll give you ladies some privacy," Papa said and snuck out.

The next twenty minutes were spent by Grams helping me to undress and gently wiping the ash and soot from my face, as well as the rest of my body.

She shook her head. "Amazing."

"What?" I asked.

"That you weren't burned. You don't even have any scratches."

Perhaps I was part cat and had nine lives. I'd escaped death three times already. Hopefully I didn't have six more life-threatening events looming in my future.

When I was clean, Grams helped me to slip on the gown. She then grabbed a comb from her purse and carefully ran it through my singed hair. Her gentleness throughout all of it calmed my soul and made my heart sing with love for her. I grabbed her hand and lifted it to my lips, giving the back of it a soft kiss.

"What was that for?" she asked.

"Because I love you."

She leaned forward, pressing her lips to my forehead. "I love you too, sweetheart."

THOUGH I'D ONLY HAD a sponge bath, I felt like a new woman to have my dirty, torn clothes off. Not that the hospital gown was very comfortable, but it was better than sitting in soiled clothing that served as a reminder to the event that had occurred.

My back was starting to feel better, but it was most likely because of the pain reliever I'd been given. The day was long, which meant the night would be even longer. Every time I closed my eyes I saw the dilated eyes of the Rogues, the Rogue leader tempting me to join him in the fire, or the fire itself. I had enough horrific images stored in my brain from the last seven months to cause permanent insomnia.

As night fell, Grams and Papa remained by side. "You guys should go on home. Get some rest," I mumbled through the oxygen mask.

Papa shook his head. "Nope. We're staying right here."

I glanced around the tight room. "There's nowhere for you to sleep. And there's only one chair."

"We'll get another one," Grams said. "Or I'll sit on Papa's lap if I have to."

Papa winked at her. "I wouldn't mind." He plopped down on the chair and patted his knee. "It's ready for ya."

Grams shot him a flirty look and sauntered over to him, easing onto his leg.

Papa mockingly cried out. "Goodness gracious, woman."

She slapped him on the shoulder, feigning offense.

Those two. So much love between them. Would I ever have that? My heart dropped as I realized it would never be with Liam.

CHAPTER THIRTY

I DIDN'T SLEEP A WINK IN the hospital. No surprise there. However, it wasn't only because my angst kept me awake. The beep and whir of medical machines, nurses coming in and out of the room, and the snoring of my grandparents sleeping on a cot made it impossible to get any shut eye.

By the time I was discharged, I felt such relief. I loathed hospitals. I'd been in them for one reason or another far too many times within the last few months. I'd be glad if I never had to set foot in one again.

My discharge nurse had given me a set of black scrubs to wear out of the hospital since the clothes I'd come in with were ruined and the hospital gown was a little too drafty for the wintry air. I was given a clean bill of health and told to take it easy for a few days and to drink plenty of fluids.

Papa wheeled me out of the hospital slowly, as though I were the most fragile thing in the world. He asked every five seconds if I was doing okay. I should have been asking him that same question. His coloring was off, and he looked exhausted. Would the stress of all that had occurred cause him to relapse?

We stopped at the curb and Papa handed the wheelchair duties over to Grams so he could drive the truck around.

"He's going to be overly helpful, isn't he?" I asked Grams.

She snorted. "Of course. Would you expect any less?"

"I suppose not."

Moments later, Papa stopped the truck in front of us. He slid out of the driver's seat, coming to my aid. Ever so carefully, he helped me out of the chair and practically lifted me into the passenger seat. After I was situated in the most comfortable position possible, Grams crawled in after me. The ride home wasn't as agonizing as it'd been in the ambulance. The doctor had prescribed a rather powerful painkiller, and now my back only felt tight.

When we reached the farm, Papa exited the truck and came to the passenger side. He and Grams helped me to gracelessly slide out. With my grandparents on either side of me, we cautiously walked up the porch steps. Inside, they guided me to my room where Grams assisted me into a pair of sweats and a T-shirt. Then they both helped me to the living room where I was lowered onto the couch and encouraged to lay down.

"Would you like a pillow?" Papa asked.

"Not for my head. But for my feet would be nice."

Papa grabbed a cushion and placed it beneath my ankles.

Grams left us for a moment and headed to the kitchen, bringing a glass of water with her when she returned. She placed it on the table beside the sofa. Papa snagged the afghan off the back of the couch and covered me with it.

"What else do you need, sweet pea?"

"Nothing. I'm good. Thank you both so much."

"Would you like the TV on?" Grams asked.

"Sure."

Grams grabbed the remote, flipping on the television. The local news played, and it took me a minute to realize that the image on the screen was of what remained of our church. The pile of charred and blackened wood was once a place of worship. Now it was nothing.

A sob caught in Grams' throat.

The same reporter from before appeared on the screen. Wasn't she tired of reporting these tragedies? I was tired of not only hearing about them, but also living them.

"There were only minor injuries thanks to the courageous

efforts of one the church's attendees, Nina Anderson." The picture the media had used of me during the trial appeared in a box in the right-hand corner. The screen then went to an interview with Pastor Johnson.

"If it wasn't for Nina, I wouldn't be standing here today." His eyes filled with tears. "She investigated the crawl space, created a hole in the concrete wall big enough for people to fit through, and guided the members to safety."

Grams and Papa looked at me, pride glowing on their faces. They shouldn't be proud. They should be disgusted with the fact that it was because of me that it occurred in the first place.

Pastor Johnson continued. "The church is only a building. We can continue to worship and love our God. And the fact that everybody escaped unharmed is all that matters."

It *was* all that mattered, but the fire wouldn't have happened if it wasn't for me.

THE DAY WAS SPENT being lazier than I'd ever been, with my grandparents at my beck and call even if I didn't ask for anything. By the afternoon, I was tired of daytime television, and my painkillers were making me sleepy.

I started to pull myself up, but Papa was by my side forcing me back down. "What do you need, sweet pea? I'll get it for you."

"I think I'll take a nap."

Grams yawned. "Good idea. I might take one as well."

Unfortunately, even as exhausted as I was, I knew I wasn't going to be able to sleep. But I might as well not keep Grams and Papa from some much-needed rest.

Papa helped me to sit up and pulled me to my feet. He and Grams followed behind as I shuffled to my bedroom and carefully crawled into bed.

Grams tucked the covers beneath my chin and kissed me on the forehead. "Sleep well, dear."

"Thanks, Grams."

Papa leaned down and kissed my cheek. "Can I get you anything else?"

"I'm okay. Thanks for everything."

The two shot me sweet smiles as they exited the room, closing the door behind them. I stared up at the ceiling. Sleep evaded me as I knew it would. Not because of the pain in my back—it had faded to a dull ache as though I'd done a tough workout. Instead, images from the fire kept me awake, and the terror on the churchgoers' faces flashed through my mind. I threw my arm over my eyes.

Restlessness was going to be the death of me. Cabin fever had set in long ago. I needed to get out of the house. I didn't need to go far. Just to the barn to visit the horses. Ugh, but Papa and Grams wouldn't approve. I flopped over to my side and released a loud sigh. No, I couldn't go outside. Not after what happened yesterday. But was I going to stay indoors until the passage was destroyed? What if that took months?

I sat up slowly and glanced out my window. The afternoon sun summoned me to come into the fresh air. I puffed up my cheeks and let it out slowly. I couldn't live my life in fear. I wouldn't allow the enemy to dictate how I was going to live my life. He wanted me to be afraid. He wanted me to cower. I couldn't give him that satisfaction.

I pounded my fist on the bed as I made my decision. I wouldn't be gone long. Ten minutes tops. I got out of bed and grabbed my coat, sliding my arms into the sleeves. I tiptoed to my door, opening it carefully. It squeaked deafeningly and I grimaced, waiting to see if I could hear my grandparents' snores. At the end of the hall, they sawed logs louder than a lumberjack.

Tiptoeing, I made it to the kitchen and to the back porch where I slipped on my boots. A thin layer of powder still covered the ground, but thankfully no ice remained. I'd still need to take it slow getting to the barn, but at least I didn't have the added danger of slipping.

On my trek down the path, I kept a wary eye on my surroundings, but also tried to soak up the sun. Not a cloud was visible in the bright blue sky. When the sky was this clear, and the wind still enough that every small sound echoed, it was then I felt closest to heaven. Amazing how such simple, mundane things could make one ponder life and the existence of God.

When bad things happened, it was easy to wonder about His existence. How could a God who loves us so much allow such horrible things to occur? I'd come to realize that God didn't allow evil to happen. Because humans were created with free will, they could choose a life of evil or a life of good. But, if a person chose a life of evil, was it too late? Could somebody taken over by a Rogue be redeemed?

I reached the barn and slid open the heavy door. Hezzie and Hazel whinnied as I flipped on the light. I slid the door closed behind me and locked it from the inside, just in case. A part of me was skeptical about whether both horses were truly standing before me. Were they hallucinations? How would I know? Again, I couldn't continue to live my life in fear.

I approached the horses' pens, and Hezzie stuck his nose out through the slats, nudging me in the chest. "I missed you too, buddy. It's been a long couple of days." I caressed the diamond between his eyes.

My mind couldn't help but wander to Liam. I'd thought our love was strong enough to endure any obstacle, but I never expected this type of difficulty. It was going to take a long time for my heart to quit loving him.

I could only hope he wasn't angry with me. He had to understand. He knew how hard it was. The only way it truly could work was if Liam became human. The only way that was possible was if a Rogue had control of his soul. It hadn't worked out for Julian. No doubt it wouldn't work out for Liam either.

We would forever have been at an impasse. No way to grow in our relationship because of the restrictions. "It was for the best," I said out loud, trying to reassure myself.

A knock sounded at the stable door. My heart leapt into my throat.

"Nina!" Grams called from the other side. Her voice held panic.

"I'm okay, Grams." I rushed to the door to unlock it. "Sorry I left the house. I couldn't be cooped up any longer."

I slid open the door to find Grams without a coat, her eyes wide with fear. "Grams!" I wrapped an arm around her shoulder, guiding her into the barn. "You're going to freeze to death."

She shook her head, stepping away from my grip. "It's your grandfather. He woke from his nap saying he was going to split wood. I had a bad feeling so I went to the field." Her voice wavered. "Nina, he wasn't there."

Why would he choose to split wood now? He didn't have enough strength yet to do such a strenuous activity. "Did he say he was going anywhere else?"

She shook her head. "The truck is still out front. He has to be on foot."

I joined Grams outside and slid the door shut behind me. "He can't be very far."

Grams took off ahead of me, heading for the trail leading beside the lagoon.

"Wait, we need to get you a coat."

She glanced back at me briefly. "There's no time. Come on!"

She walked briskly, not seeming to be fazed by the below freezing temperature. Where could Papa have gone? And why would he go anywhere at such a dangerous time?

We reached the small clearing behind the lagoon. The stump Papa used as a pedestal to split the logs was empty. No logs had been cut. The axe was nowhere in sight. And most importantly,

Papa was absent. And strangely, no footprints led to or surrounded the log. Papa must not have come out here at all.

Grams glanced briefly at the spot where Papa should have been before taking off again.

"Grams, wait!"

Somehow she was already at least a hundred yards past the lagoon. How in the world did she move so fast?

"Grams!" I ran after her, but I couldn't gain any ground. She seemed to get farther and farther away the faster I ran.

I glanced behind me. We'd traveled far enough away that the farmhouse couldn't be seen. When I turned back around, Grams was even farther ahead. How was she doing this? Was it possible a Martyr was helping somehow?

"Grams, wait!"

Grams slowed slightly and looked over her shoulder. "I see footprints. He went this way."

Why would he have gone off on his own? Especially when he knew what kind of danger lurked around here. My eyes widened as it dawned on me. He was out looking for the passage too.

I increased my speed and the wind suddenly picked up, bringing with it a sharp chill. A cornfield loomed ahead and Grams disappeared into it. When I reached it, I bent over as I caught my breath, ignoring the ache shooting through my back. I didn't have long to rest. How did Grams not need a break?

I stepped in to the field, the crunchy wet stalks gripped my clothes as though begging me to stay. Running through it was nearly impossible. With each step, my boots sucked into the mud. With nothing to grip to help me escape the hold, I had to rely on my own will and strength to free my feet.

The trek was long and messy. My hair had been pulled from its ponytail, the bottom of my sweats were caked in mud, and nearly every inch of me was soaked through. My teeth chattered. Where was Grams? Had she made it out?

"Grams?" With one last step, I was suddenly out of the field. What I saw next made my jaw drop in awe. A cluster of weeping willows stood before me. Their already droopy branches sagged further because of the ice that weighed them down. And with the sun shining off of them, they seemed to sparkle.

I stepped forward, reaching out to sweep my hand across the branches. They tinkled like wind chimes. A gust of wind swept through, causing the branches to clang against each other. A beautiful chorus of bells ensued.

The noise mesmerized me enough to make me forget what I was doing. I shook my head, gazing through the trees. Grams stood not too far ahead in the midst of the frozen trees.

"Grams!" I called again, but she didn't turn around.

She kept her gaze trained forward. What was she looking at? I stepped over fallen branches and protruding roots. I reached Grams, coming up beside her cautiously. Her cheeks were rosy, but she didn't look cold, and she wasn't breathing as if she'd almost ran two miles.

"Grams?"

She turned toward me. "I'm so worried. Where is he?" She grabbed my shoulders and pulled me into a hug.

I closed my eyes and buried my cold nose into her neck, breathing in deeply. My eyes shot open. Why didn't she smell like lemons?

I shoved away from her, stepping out of the embrace. My chest heaved on sharp inhalations.

She cocked her head. "What's the matter, dear?" she said with a deep voice that was far from my grandmother's.

I took another step back. "Who are you?"

My heart pounded. Oh no. Had I fallen for another hallucination? I glanced behind me. Only one set of footprints led to where we stood. And they were mine.

I turned to whoever or whatever stood before me. She smiled eerily. Then ever so slowly, her form began to disappear until I was alone. I spun around, glancing every which way. It wasn't her. Grams hadn't been here. I'd chased a hallucination for miles. Were she and Papa still safe in the farmhouse?

Lord, please let them be okay.

I had to get away from this place. Whatever the reason I'd been lured here, I wouldn't allow myself to be led into a trap. I spun around to leave the mystical, frozen forest, but I literally couldn't move. My feet felt glued to the ground. I attempted to turn my neck, but it was stuck as well. I opened my mouth to yell for help, but my lips wouldn't part. My entire body was paralyzed. I was a prisoner in my own body, and I couldn't escape.

The only things I could move were my eyes. I shifted them from side to side. Was this even real? Were my surroundings truly here? I pinched my eyes shut, willing the trees to disappear. Praying I would open my eyes and be back in the barn safe and sound.

One, two, three, open.

If I had been able to scream, it would have echoed through the woods.

CHAPTER THIRTY-ONE

MY NOSTRILS FLARED AND MY CHEST rose and fell on panicked breaths. The man in black who'd been haunting my dreams as well as haunting me while awake, stood a few yards in front of me. It was him. The Rogue leader.

The black hood of his trench coat concealed his face. His gloved hands were in fists down by sides. But the most peculiar thing was the blue fog rising from the ground where he stood. The mist swirled above and beside him.

Every muscle in my body ached as I tried desperately to get them to move. Sweat budded on my forehead. Why had he led me here? What did he want from me?

"Come," he said with a gravelly voice. "I want to show you something."

How? I couldn't move. Even if I could, I wouldn't follow him.

My muscles suddenly relaxed, and I no longer felt ensnared. I spun around, ready to dart in the other direction. The moment I took a step forward, I became paralyzed once again.

"No, Nina. You want to follow me."

My body relaxed and I could move again. Instead of running away, I turned around, facing him once again. Wait, what was I doing? I had to get away.

"Follow me." He turned and began walking with a gait so silent I wasn't sure if his feet touched the ground. The blue swirls followed him as if he were their source of life.

A part of my brain begged me to flee, but a more dominate

part wouldn't allow me to. I took a step forward. Then another. I continued until I matched the tempo of his steps.

Turn around and run!

No, keep following him. You know you want to.

A war waged in my mind between two parts of my brain, as though two sentient beings were fighting for control over my actions. What did he want to show me? Could he have the answer to all of my problems?

I don't know how long we walked. Long enough for a grey fog to roll in, hovering over the ground like smoke. The man didn't check to see if I was still behind him. He continued on with determination for whatever destination lay in wait for us.

The Rogue leader suddenly stopped. I stopped as well. "Come stand beside me, Nina," he said without looking back at me.

I did as he said, moving to his side. A thick wall of fog blocked us from going any further. The man raised his hands, pointing them toward the fog. He separated his hands slowly and the wall split, creating an opening big enough to pass through.

A dilapidated wooden shack stood in front of us. The roof hung cockeyed with gaping holes through the wooden shingles. The two windows on either side of the door contained no glass, and the planks that remained on the porch looked as though they were decaying.

"What is this?" I asked.

"What you've been looking for." The blue mist left the man, disappearing through the windows.

The passage! It had been here all along? Practically in my grandparents' backyard?

"Go on in," he said.

No! Don't go inside!

Yes, go. You know you're curious.

I stepped forward, then glanced behind me. The Rogue leader stood unmoving. This was crazy. I couldn't go in alone. But a part of me wanted to go inside. Tentatively, I put weight on the rickety stairs leading up to the porch. They creaked and snapped loudly. Maybe this wasn't such a good idea.

I looked over my shoulder again. The Rogue leader was gone. Now was my chance to escape.

Run! Run now!

No. Go inside.

I faced the door and nodded. It would only take two steps to get to the door. Would the porch hold me? Perhaps, if I walked quickly. With a short breath, I stepped lightly across the worn wood, making it safely to the threshold. I reached for the knob, and the door opened on its own.

I entered the dark shack, and the door slammed behind me. Lights flickered on from lanterns hanging on the narrow walls. My breath left my lungs. How was this possible? The state of the interior of the shack did not at all reflect the outside.

A long, ornate rug covered the black, pristine wood floor leading to a winding staircase made of marble. Atop ivory pillars encasing the first step were gold candelabras, lit with a blue flame. How could this place have more than one floor?

I glanced around the small entryway. No other doors. The only way to go was up. I planted my foot on the first stair. What would I find when I reached the top? How far was it to the top? I craned my neck, searching for the end. The length of the stairs disappeared into a dark unknown. I swallowed hard.

Turn around!

Keep going.

I squared my shoulders and grabbed hold of the wrought iron railing, then lifted my foot to the next step. The same part of my brain that insisted this was wrong nagged at the back of my mind, but I ignored it and continued up the stairs. I had to know what was up there.

The stairs wound around once and I thought that was the end, until it twisted a second time, a third time, and I lost count after five. The muscles in my thighs protested, and my heaving lungs begged me to stop. But I couldn't. As though I were on autopilot, I kept my eyes trained ahead and continued to climb.

A smell began to permeate the air, becoming stronger the higher I went. I lifted my nose, sniffing. Was that sulfur? What was that sound? Music? It was soft. So soft I had to strain my ears to hear it. A piano, playing a slow melody. It was soothing. How bad could a place be if it created such beautiful sounds?

Right when I thought the staircase had no end, a landing appeared out of nowhere. The piano I'd heard stood at the top of the stairs. It played on its own, as though a ghost were pressing the keys. Two double steels doors were beyond the piano. An intricate overlay of ivy made of gold spread across the doors, but no handle or knob were present. How was I supposed to get inside?

Leave now!

My teeth snatched my bottom lip. I looked over my shoulder toward the stairs. Even if I wanted to leave, I couldn't. A wall had replaced the stairs. The only other thing in the small room with me was the piano, which continued to play. The only place for me to go was through the door.

Go in. Now.

But how? I reached out, touching the tips of my fingers to the ivy. It glistened and stirred as though it were alive. With a gasp, I pulled my hand back. Things here weren't what they seemed. What caused this distorted reality? Sorcery of some kind?

Tentatively, I reached for the ivy again, placing my hand directly on it. It shimmered as it did before, and the vines vibrated. The leaves lifted away from the door and draped themselves across my hand, the vines intertwining with my fingers. A wince escaped my lips as the ivy squeezed. What was it doing?

Slowly, the ivy uncoiled itself from my hand. All the vines unattached themselves from the door and slid away like snakes, slithering up the ceiling, along the wall, and to the floor. The steel doors popped open slightly. The piano's melody suddenly stopped.

Now or never. I took a deep breath and pushed open the doors. My heart stopped.

CHAPTER THIRTY-TWO

LIAM KICKED AT THE CHARRED DEBRIS of the church, looking for something he could have missed the last time he was there. He'd been sifting through the burned beams and fragments of debris all night. But he had yet to discover a clue.

The rescue crews had found the remains of the people who had been taken over by the Rogues. Even if he'd had a chance to examine the bodies, he wouldn't have known what to look for.

He'd have to continue the search blind. But being tricked during his previous search caused him to be extra paranoid. It would be hard to know if he was being deceived again.

"Liam," Kimmie said behind him.

He spun around to find Damian and Violet on either side of her. They stared at the wreckage in disbelief. He hadn't seen any of them since the fire occurred. He squinted, trying to determine if they were a hallucination. "Where have you all been?"

Damian stepped forward. "We were lost in the forest. The leader cast an illusion."

Kimmie nodded. "Damian was tricked into thinking he was following me and I him. Violet thought she was with you."

Liam released a sigh. "It happened to me as well. I was able to find my way out because I heard Nina calling for me."

Kimmie fanned her hands out. "He led us away so that he could do this?" Tears filled her eyes. "What a monster."

"Were there any casualties?" Damian asked.

"Only the folks who were influenced by a Rogue."

Kimmie wiped at her eyes. "Is Nina okay?"

Liam couldn't help but smile. His strong, heroic Nina. So fearless. "It's because of Nina that everybody is alive."

And once again, he'd been almost too late to save her. He was starting to believe she truly was better off without him. He'd failed her on more than one occasion. Some protector he was.

Violet signed to the group.

Liam shook his head. "No. I don't want to rest. I need to keep searching."

Kimmie came to him, gently touching his arm. "We all need to rest. Let's go to the clearing for a few hours, make a new plan, and we'll search together. This time, we won't split up."

Liam rubbed his palm over his face. She was right. He was exhausted. If he wanted a chance at finding the passage, then he needed a clear head.

CHAPTER THIRTY-THREE

THE DOORS OPENED TO THE NEVER-ending hallway from my nightmare where bare purple walls stretched for miles. What was this place?

Don't go any further!

Step into the hallway.

My feet obeyed the second part of my brain. I didn't want to glance down. I knew what I'd find, but at the same time I needed to be sure. I closed my eyes briefly before looking to the glass floor below me. Green snakes of varying sizes slithered along the underside. Their tongues shot out of their mouths, smelling the glass.

My palms grew sweaty as the snakes thickened under my feet. One particular snake with red, beady eyes stared directly at me. It opened its mouth wide, baring its sharp fangs. They dripped with venom. It drew its neck back and launched at the glass. A dull thud echoed through the hall.

A shiver shook my body, and I tipped my head upward. As I expected, the ceiling was absent. Grey clouds swirled around the space. In a moment, one would form into some sort of beast. I wouldn't allow myself to watch it happen.

I trained my eyes straight ahead, readying myself for the next part of the dream. The painted portraits and mirrors now lined the walls. I walked forward slowly. My gaze drifted across the paintings to my left. I'd never noticed any of the other people within the pictures before. Old, young, male, female, black, white. I couldn't find a similarity other than every face held the saddest expression. Who were they? Why were their pictures here?

I stopped when I reached the little boy. His black hair fell over his droopy brown eyes. His thin lips pulled down into a frown. I reached toward the boy, tracing my fingertips along his cheek.

"Hello?" I whispered.

He remained motionless. Oh, yes. He wouldn't say anything until I approached the triangle mirror. I spun around, finding the large mirror behind me. As always, my reflection wasn't there. I stretched my fingers out toward the glass.

"Don't!" the little boy cried behind me.

I glanced at him over my shoulder.

He blinked, then tilted his head to peer around me.

I returned my attention to the mirror. As expected, my reflection was now present. Only it wasn't me. This woman was so much more beautiful. Her hair was a shade of red I could only dream of possessing. And her vivid green eyes seemed to glitter. Exactly like in my dream, the most attractive thing about her was the fact that no scar marred her neck. Her rosy lips pulled into a smile. My heart ached to know this woman. To be this woman.

She suddenly disappeared.

"Wait!" I called.

The blue mist appeared and swirled behind the mirror. A shiver passed over my body. Here he comes. The man who'd led me here slowly materialized within the mist. He stalked toward me.

"Run!" the painting boy cried.

Stay.

The leader kept his head down, the black hood casting a shadow over his face. In a moment he would show me his face and throw an illusion to make himself look like Jeremy.

He lifted his head revealing ashen, soft skin. My fingers flinched by my side as I held back my desire to stroke his cheek. His icy eyes bore into mine with a mixture of lust and anger. His pale, full lips lifted into a sinister smile, revealing straight, white teeth.

Why wouldn't he show me who he really was? I swallowed hard. "Show me your true self," I demanded.

He cocked his head to the side. "This is my true self."

My eyes widened.

His gloved hand shot out of the mirror and wrapped around my throat.

CHAPTER THIRTY-FOUR

LIAM LAY ON THE FLAT OF his back, staring at the clouds passing over the clearing. This down time only caused him to think about Nina and all the things he could have done differently. Now that he was no longer with her, he couldn't hear her thoughts. He'd tried. The usual hum her thoughts created in the back of his head was absent.

His lips turned up into a smile as he imagined what life would be like with her if he were only human. He'd marry her the first chance he'd get. They'd create a family. Perhaps find a farmhouse close to her grandparents. It would be perfect.

But that wasn't possible. He couldn't offer her all of that, not without paying a horrible price. Now that she didn't want to be with him, what would he do with his time once his mission was complete? Go back home and spend his days wishing he was with Nina? Or perhaps take on one assignment after another to keep him busy.

Liam threw an arm over his eyes. Perhaps he shouldn't have volunteered to find the passage in the first place. Then Nina wouldn't have ended things with him, and they could have gone on the way things were. But he couldn't have sat by and done nothing knowing the Rogues were wreaking havoc.

He sighed. It didn't matter now. What was done was done. He couldn't change the past. He closed his eyes, imagining a human life with Nina. The life he would never have. He pushed himself to rest—worked to clear his mind and quit worrying about Nina, but something was there in the background. Not quite her thoughts but something. He sat up and looked around. Had the clearing changed?

No. It looked exactly the same as when they'd arrived. But deep inside he knew. A Rogue was on the move. Liam bolted to his feet, searching in every direction, straining to hear, trying to quiet his thudding heart. Did it have to do with Nina? No. She was home, safe with her grandparents, right? What was it, then?

CHAPTER THIRTY-FIVE

I CLUTCHED AT THE MAN'S WRIST as he pulled me toward him. He sneered as he watched his admission register in my mind.

He was Jeremy. Jeremy was the Rogue leader. But how?

His grip tightened around my throat. I sucked in a sharp breath, forcing air through my tightening airway.

"We'll get to the how," he grated. "There's plenty of time for that."

His grasp loosened slightly, and I inhaled deeply. The stench of vinegar nearly made me gag. He pulled me toward him, inching me closer to the mirror. I dragged my feet, my boots squeaking across the glass floor. Wait! I can't go through there!

But somehow I did. The glass became a jelly-like substance, and I passed through with ease. The moment I was on the other side, Jeremy released his hold. Thick blue fog swirled around us. So thick I could hardly see Jeremy. He smiled wickedly before stepping back, completely disappearing into the fog.

I whirled around frantically. He could be anywhere, ready to strike at any moment. His laugh echoed through the room, surrounding me with its wickedness. Why was he doing this?

"Because you are mine, Nina."

No! I'm not!

Yes, you are.

The fog started to scatter, revealing the small room I stood within. Before I could get a good look, the room fell dark. The hairs on the back of my neck stood on end. Sound seemed to have been sucked from the room with the fog. The only thing to be heard was a ringing in my ears and my panicked breathing.

It was so dark; I couldn't even see my hand in front of my face. Jeremy could be right behind me, and I wouldn't know. My hands curled into fists, ready to defend myself in a fight I knew I couldn't win.

"Jeremy! Stop being a coward and face me."

The floor suddenly fell out from beneath me. I let out a scream as I plunged down. My free fall continued for what felt like an eternity until I landed in freezing cold water. The icy liquid stung my skin like tiny needles.

The weight of my coat prevented me from swimming. I ripped it off and swam upward, or what I thought was up. Right when I thought I was going to surface, the water continued. The darkness surrounded me, persistently pulling me under. I couldn't tell which direction I was going.

My lungs constricted, begging me to fight for oxygen. I sliced my arms every which way, seeking the air I so desperately needed. I wasn't finding it. This was how I was going to die. In vain, I continued to swim for my life. I wasn't going to be able to hold my breath much longer. As I was about to involuntarily inhale, I was wrenched out of the water.

My mouth opened, and I sucked in air. My lungs ached and burned as they filled with oxygen. Air had never tasted so good. Whoever had pulled me out deposited me face down onto a hard surface with my legs still hanging in the water. I lifted my head enough to cough and wheeze. My hair clung to my face like seaweed.

When I regained enough strength, I pulled the rest of my body out of the water and came to my hands and knees. It was then that I realized the hard surface I'd been dragged onto was a slab of concrete.

"Much better," Jeremy's voice boomed. "You were awfully dirty."

I jerked my head up, searching for him. He was nowhere to

be seen in the small room. A single bulb hung from the ceiling of what felt like a jail cell. Concrete covered floor to ceiling. I glanced behind me. There was nothing within the room save for the pool I'd been dropped into.

How was I going to get out? And even if I did, where would it   lead? "Don't worry your pretty little head over it, Nina." This time his voice came from right in front of me.

I swiveled my head to meet his gaze. Jeremy leaned against the wall, his arms crossed with one ankle draped over the other. His hood was down, revealing his hairless pale head. Even with his ghostly, unearthly appearance, he was still handsome. My lip curled for thinking that. He wasn't handsome. He had an ugly heart. A putrid mind. A despicable soul.

Jeremy raised a sardonic brow. "You realize I can hear everything you're thinking."

"Good!" I wanted him to hear what I thought of him. But fear still gripped my backbone and quivered through my flesh.

The corner of his mouth lifted with conceit.

Arrogant man. Or was he even a man anymore? How had he become the passage leader?

He rolled his eyes. "Ask me the questions that your mind won't stop spinning."

I wouldn't give him the satisfaction of staring down at me while I remained at his mercy on the ground. I stood, trying to hide my wobbly legs, then cleared my throat. "Did you really die that day?"

He uncrossed his ankles and arms. "Yes. But I was brought back to life. Or rather, I was brought back to another type of existence."

My eyes narrowed. "By whom?"

Jeremy moved away from the wall and began slowly pacing the enclosed space. "They call him The Great Serpent, The Wicked One, The King of the Bottomless Pit to name a few. He chooses those who have all the fine qualities of leading a tribe of sadistic beings." He looked at his fingernails and buffed them on his trench coat. "He found a good one, wouldn't you say?"

That he did. Was there anyone more evil than Jeremy Winters?

I swallowed hard. "Where were you between the time you were brought back and when the passage was made? Hell?"

He lifted a brow and smirked.

Goosebumps popped up on my arms. "Why here? Why was the passage created here?"

He stopped pacing. "Oh, Nina. You should know the answer to that." He pointed to his chest. "I had my say in where to place the passage. And of course, I had to put it wherever you were."

My gut clenched. So all of this was because of me. All the fires, the murders, and other crimes were because Jeremy still wasn't done with me. Even in his death.

He grinned maliciously. "Anything I've ever done has always been for you. I told you that you'd be mine forever."

My heart dropped into my stomach. *Liam will come after me.*

"Oh, I'm banking on it that he will. Him and his three little protégés." Jeremy crossed his arms. "Does he really think he can take me out with his puny army?" He chuckled. "My original plan was only to have you, but there are certain stipulations that come with the territory of being a Rogue leader. Taking out the Martyrs being the main one," he said nonchalantly.

I was never going to win this. The Martyrs weren't going to win this. Jeremy had been powerful in his life and had become even more so in his death. None of us stood a chance. A solitary tear rolled down my cheek.

Jeremy moved forward until his toes nearly touched mine. He reached his gloved hand toward me. I held my breath and stiffened. Lightly, he wiped the tear away.

"It won't be so bad here with me, my love. Come, I'll show you." He held out his hand.

Don't touch him!
Hold his hand.

I clenched my hands by my sides, refusing to budge. I wouldn't become his slave. I couldn't. Not again. As though I had no control over my body, my hand shot out and I placed it in his.

CHAPTER THIRTY-SIX

LIAM FOUND HIMSELF IN A DARK, icy pool. His lungs ached as he tried desperately to find the surface of the water. The more he swam, the further he seemed to get from the possibility of being able to breathe. Just when he thought his lungs were going to burst, he was pulled up by the collar of his shirt.

He gulped in air as fast as he could. His body dropped onto something hard. He came to his hands and knees, coughing until his throat stung. When his breathing evened, his eyes focused on the puddle below him, seeing his reflection. But it wasn't his own. He looked up and stared directly into the pale eyes of the Rogue leader.

Jeremy.

Jeremy smiled. "Hello, Nina."

Liam jerked awake with a gasp. Eyes wide, he scanned the clearing and realized where he was. He jumped to his feet.

"What's wrong?" Kimmie asked from her pallet a few yards away.

"Nina's in trouble," he said, heading toward the trees.

Kimmie came up beside him. "Where is she?"

"The passage." But he didn't get a good enough look at her surroundings to know where that could be.

He shoved through the trees as easily as if they were made of cloth and stomped through what remained of the snow, not entirely sure where he was going.

Kimmie followed after him. "What else did you see?"

He gritted his teeth. "Jeremy."

Her brows wrinkled. "Jeremy's a Rogue?"

Liam shook his head. "He's their leader."

"How is that possible?"

"I don't know. I think there's more to Rogues than we understand." He picked up his pace. "All that matters is finding Nina."

Kimmie grabbed his arm. "Liam, you can't go after her alone. Let's wake the other two and come up with a plan."

His brows furrowed. "There isn't time for that."

She pulled at his wrist, but he didn't slow. "We need to be smart about this. You can't simply waltz into the passage and get Nina out. You could wind up getting her killed."

His heart dropped at the thought of something happening to Nina because of his stupid actions. He released a loud sigh and stopped, turning to face Kimmie. "You're right. You go wake the others and meet me at the farm."

She squeezed his hand. "We'll find her, Liam. She's going to be okay."

He wasn't so sure about that.

LET GO OF HIS hand! He is the enemy!

He's not. You know that this feels right.

My brain argued with itself as I held onto Jeremy's gloved hand, seemingly against my will. I sought out what my heart felt. It seemed to have been shut down momentarily, as it gave me no answers.

Jeremy headed straight for the concrete wall of the jail cell. Would he pull me through it just as he tugged me through the mirror?

He swept his hand flippantly, and a vertical crack shot down the middle of the wall. Moments later, the concrete separated enough for us to pass through. I glanced behind us when we exited the room. The wall pieced back together, and the crack disappeared.

Jeremy led me down a wide hallway so very different from the one I'd been in before. This one had marble floors with red swirls that reminded me of blood. The ceiling consisted of gold chandeliers, while the grey walls held sconces and artwork that belonged in a museum.

"Who are those people in the portraits of the purple hallway?" I asked.

He rubbed at his chin with his free hand. "Aw, great question. Those are all the souls currently being ruled by Rogues from this passage."

That child had been taken over by a Rogue? Did anybody, no matter the age, have the capacity to choose evil? "Yes," Jeremy answered my unspoken question.

I swallowed hard. "What are the mirrors?"

"Each has a different role. Some are merely there as décor. Others are entrances to different parts of my palace."

I had to hold back a snort. His palace? He was a king?

"Indeed I am."

"What was the mirror that I've been looking at?

"You'll find out soon enough."

My heart pounded. "Where are you taking me?"

"To show you what could be yours."

We reached an arched door that stretched from floor to ceiling. Spread across the surface were strange symbols and letters I imagined one would find within an old cave. I recognized only one. A circle with a five-pointed star in the middle. A shiver crawled up my spine.

Jeremy released my hand and gestured toward the knob. "Ladies first."

I stepped in and my jaw dropped.

CHAPTER THIRTY-SEVEN

LIAM AND THE THREE OTHER MARTYRS sat around the dining table in the farmhouse. Nina's grandparents paced the room as they absorbed all the information Liam had told them—and he'd told them everything. Every detail from the day he was first placed, to all that he knew about Rogues, up to the current situation.

They were wasting precious time, but he had to let Stephen and Jaynie know. They were both understandably distraught. Jaynie had broken down in tears when she rushed to Nina's room to find her bed vacant.

Jaynie twirled the end of her braid. "You haven't found the passage yet?"

"No," Liam answered.

"And you know for certain that's where Nina is?" Stephen asked.

"Yes."

Tears filled Jaynie's eyes. "Did Jeremy sneak into the house and take her?"

"That's what we're looking into," Kimmie answered. "Did she say anything before she lay down?"

Jaynie shook her head. "She was getting tired of being in the house. She could have gone out to the barn since she hadn't seen the horses in a couple of days. But she should have known that it was too dangerous."

"That's never stopped her before," Liam said dryly. "But Jeremy could have created a hallucination to draw her away. He did the same to all of us."

Stephen released a defeated sigh. "What can we do?"

"Stay in the house. Don't let anybody in. Even if you know them. You don't know if it could be an illusion." Liam stood, ready to start his search. Every minute they wasted was another minute that Nina could be getting closer to being hurt or . . . lost forever.

Jaynie came to him, wrapping her arms around his waist. "Please bring her back safely."

He patted her on the back and nodded. Even if it destroyed him, he would bring Nina back.

IN MY LIFE, I had never seen anything designed so beautifully, but this room left my heart cold. A tile floor encrusted with diamonds led into a room so luxurious that Cleopatra would have cried with envy. Crystal chandeliers hung from a ceiling with a painted mural I imagined Michelangelo could have created. Ivory columns reminiscent of an ancient cathedral lined the red carpet leading to a three-step platform where a Tudor-style throne rested. The high-back chair sang of elegance with its dark oak wood and blue velvet cushions.

Was this Jeremy's throne? The chair on which he sat upon to watch his minions do his dirty work?

Jeremy's lips touched my ear. "No, no, Nina. This is your throne."

I cringed away from the contact. What did he mean?

"Let me show you."

He gripped my waist and steered me toward the throne. My boots left wet prints along the carpet that was probably worth more than my grandparents' house. We reached the throne, and it was then that I realized a fire crackled from the hearth behind it.

"Go ahead," Jeremy said. "Have a seat."

"But my clothes are wet."

"No they're not."

I looked down and gasped. My soggy sweats and T-shirt had somehow been replaced with an exquisite silk gown edged with a purple damask print. Lace covered the full skirt and the Victorian corset glittered with jewels.

"How did you do this?" I whispered.

"Not to worry. Please. Have a seat."

What would happen if I sat on it? What kind of trick waited for me?

"No tricks."

Don't sit on it!

Do as he says.

Something seemed to push me forward. I grabbed hold of my skirt and lifted, finding on my feet a pair of glass high heels like Cinderella wore. I took the steps carefully, eyeing the throne. Horned beasts protruded from the arms of the chair. I trailed my fingers across a wooden fang, and then turned around, coming face-to-face with Jeremy who had followed me up the steps. He held the triangle mirror from the purple hallway.

"What is that for?"

"Sit and you shall see."

No! Don't!

Yes. Sit.

Something made me obey the second part of my brain, easing onto the cushion. Jeremy held the mirror directly in front of me. My reflection made me sneer. Bloodshot eyes stared back at me. My drab, lifeless hair hung wet on my shoulders. I didn't belong in this beautiful dress.

"Yes, you do," Jeremy whispered. "Look closer."

The change was gradual, but apparent. First, my pale skin flushed to a healthy bronze. Then, my eyes cleared and brightened to a beautiful jade. Next, my hair transformed to a vibrant red hue, filling with volume and bounce. Lastly, the ghastly scar on my neck disappeared.

I reached up, tracing my fingertips where my scar used to be. It was gone! But wait. It was this man who stood before who had caused the scar. Now he was taking it away? It didn't make sense. What was the catch?

"See how beautiful you are?" Jeremy said. "This could be you." He looked around the throne room. "All of this can be yours. You can have anything you want with the snap of your fingers."

Nothing is worth this!

Yes it is. Listen to him.

"You belong with me, Nina. You are mine. Admit it and you can have everything you've always wanted."

Don't say it!

Say it. Now.

Jeremy set down the mirror and moved closer, dropping to his knees in front of me. "Tell me, Nina. You know you love me. Tell me you are mine."

No, don't say it!

My mouth opened against my will. I looked him straight in the eye. "I am yours."

CHAPTER THIRTY-EIGHT

THE FOOTPRINTS THAT BEGAN AT THE barn led behind the farmhouse to the lagoon, circled around a log-splitting stump, and then continued.

Violet's brows rose, and she signed to Liam.

Liam shook his head. "I thought of that too, Violet. I don't think Jeremy faked these prints. I smell jasmine among these tracks. Nina was here."

Kimmie glanced around. "What type of illusion could have lured her out here?"

"It had to have been something she cared deeply about."

Damian pointed behind the lagoon. "Her tracks continue this way."

"Let's go," Liam said.

The four of them took off, using their talent of speed to follow Nina's prints without taking a pause. They darted through the corn field, coming to a halt when they reached the willows.

Thick, grey fog swirled before them in the forest.

Liam turned to his allies. "Be on alert."

He led the way, eyes darting back and forth. He had to be ready for anything. Jeremy could create any type of hallucination. Would Liam be able to tell if it was real or not?

Every snap of a twig or brush of the wind caused Liam's senses to be on overdrive. His hands remained in fists by his sides. He didn't usually condone violence, but when it came to Nina, he would do anything to protect her.

"Liam!" Nina's voice rang out.

His eyes widened, and he jerked his head to the right where the sound had come from.

"Liam, it may not be her," Kimmie warned.

"But what if it is?" She was calling for him. He had to go.

"Liam!" She called again. This time it came from the left.

He stopped walking. He closed his eyes, focusing all his energy on trying to reach Nina's mind. Sweat trickled down his brow. He couldn't find her. Which meant that wasn't her voice.

His eyes opened. "It isn't her. Keep going."

The voice called out multiple times, each one filled with more desperation. The last one ended with a blood-curdling scream, and he almost took off to find the source. But that was exactly what Jeremy wanted. A way to throw him off the scent. Manipulate his mind enough to make him question everything and therefore become more fallible. He couldn't allow that. He needed his mind sound enough to make rational decisions.

The deeper they went into the forest, the foggier it became. He didn't know what to look for that could be the passage. Would they even be able to see the passage through the fog?

Kimmie's hand clamped down on his wrist. "Stop." The four of them halted. Though they all shared the same powers, some of those powers were stronger within each of them. While Liam's was strength, Kimmie's was her sense of sight. Violet's was smell and Damian's was speed.

"What do you see?" Liam asked.

Kimmie squinted. "Rogues."

Damian stepped forward. "How many?"

"At least a dozen, maybe more."

"Be ready," Liam said. The foursome moved forward slowly.

While the Rogues caused the body they inhabited to be stronger than the average human, their strength didn't match that of a Martyr's. Still, four against twelve wouldn't be an easy feat. Liam hated the idea of having to kill to stop the Rogues. But what other choice did they have? Could there be another way?

Dark figures took shape a few yards away, standing their ground. They guarded something. What was it?

"Fan out. And watch your back," Liam instructed.

The four formed a line, keeping their eyes peeled for any surprise attacks. They stepped through a thick wall of fog, coming face to face with the small army of Rogues. Directly beyond them was an old shack that barely stood. That was the passage? It wasn't at all what he expected.

Liam returned his attention to the group, scanning the dozen faces staring at him with malice. He realized that nobody was safe from the influence of a Rogue. Old, young, men, women, varying races all stood before them. The youngest was a little boy of about eight with black hair. His dilated eyes stared directly at Liam. How was Liam expected to hurt an innocent child? The boy had chosen evil which allowed the Rogue in, but couldn't he change? He couldn't be too far gone. None of these people were past saving.

"Don't kill them," Liam whispered.

"What?" Damian asked.

"If at all possible, try not to harm them."

One of the men at the front of the pack snarled and charged, with the rest of the army following. Three different attackers came at Liam. They threw punches and kicks, but Liam dodged or blocked each one. They performed this dance until ordinary men and women would have grown tired, but they kept going. Too much time was wasted. Liam caught a glimpse of the other Martyrs. They too were getting nowhere. It was time to make a move.

Intending only to incapacitate, Liam used a combination of his strength and speed to drive the palm of his hand into the chest of each of his foes. The action left them sprawled out on the ground confused. The other Martyrs followed suit, leaving their assailants stunned on the ground.

They had to move fast. What could they use to secure them

before they were no longer dazed? Liam glanced around. There had to be some kind of cording, twine, or string of some sort.

Of course! Liam cleared snow from a patch of ground, revealing the soil below. He knelt and held his hands over the mud. Closing his eyes, he dug deep for his center, concentrating his power on bringing forth life from the ground.

He opened his eyes and watched a green bud snake up from the ground, growing taller and thicker by the second. Before long, a vine as tall as a two-story house stood over him.

Liam looked to his group. "Gather the Rogues together. Place them around that tree."

Damian, Kimmie, and Violet threw a Rogue over each of their shoulders, depositing their limp bodies at the base of a large tree. Liam grabbed hold of the bottom of the vine and pulled, ripping it from the ground.

Damian grabbed hold of the other end, and the two wrapped the vine around the group of Rogues that circled the tree. Liam tied the ends of the vine together, ensnaring their assailants. As the Rogues regained their strength, they struggled against the bonds, but the vine proved to be too strong. Hopefully it would be enough to hold for some time.

"I want the three of you to stay here and stand guard," Liam said.

Kimmie whipped her head in his direction. "No. We're coming with you."

He shook his head. "If they happen to break free, the three of you will be sorely needed."

"What if you need us in there?" Damian asked, tipping his head toward the shack.

Liam looked at the run-down house. He didn't know what obstacles he would encounter, but he needed to do this on his own. He couldn't put the others at risk.

He shifted his gaze to his team. "Thank you all for your help. But I can't let you get hurt over something that is part of my doing."

Violet came to him, reaching up to lightly touch his cheek. She didn't need to use sign language to tell him what she was thinking.

He smiled down at her. "I'll be careful."

Damian patted him on the shoulder. "You come back to us with your Nina."

Liam nodded.

Kimmie approached him last. She held back tears as she pulled him into a tight hug. "Be smart in there."

He returned the hug. "I will." Kimmie released the embrace first, swiping at the tears running down her cheeks.

Liam walked cautiously to the porch of the shack. The wood snapped and creaked beneath his feet. With a quick breath, he opened the door.

CHAPTER THIRTY-NINE

As Liam stepped into the shack, he imagined Nina's reaction to seeing such extravagance. She would have been in disbelief that a beautiful place could exist within an ugly exterior. Jeremy must have used his powers of persuasion to convince her to step foot in this place. She may have been curious, but she wouldn't have gone in of her own accord. She had to have had a push.

Liam mashed his lips together. If Jeremy had hurt her in any way . . . he shook his head, ridding his mind of anything that Jeremy could have possibly done to Nina.

He moved to the bottom of the marble staircase that Nina surely stared at in awe. He planted his foot on the first step and glanced around, straining his ears. Jeremy had to know he was here. Getting to Nina wasn't going to be easy. Though Liam had never experienced a passage to The In-between, he knew there were tricks and that things weren't always what they seemed. He had to be extra cautious.

He took another step, and another, stopping between each to check for a trap. By the twelfth stair, nothing had occurred. Perhaps it was going to be easier than he thought. Piano music suddenly pierced the air, the melody loud and frantic. Liam's heart raced to the tempo.

Out of nowhere, a horrible series of pops echoed through the stairwell. Liam glanced behind him. His heart sank. With each pop, a stair that he'd already conquered crumbled into dust, dropping into the black space below.

He raced up the stairs, the popping sound gaining speed as he did. The higher he climbed, the more the stairwell stretched on as though it didn't have an end. He looked behind him briefly. The stair directly below dissolved and disappeared. He wasn't going to make it. Wait! A landing lay straight ahead. Just a few more stairs and he'd be there.

The stair he was on gave way. With a growl, Liam leapt forward, extending his arms and legs as he reached for something to grab on to. His fingertips met the edge of the landing, and he grabbed hold with all his might, his legs swinging in the air.

Sulfur invaded his nose, and he glanced down. Purple and blue flames swirled beneath him, forming into tendrils that reached for his feet. As the flames inched closer, he lifted himself up to the landing, rolling onto his back and away from the ledge.

He got to his feet right away. Sweat rolled down his temples as he attempted to slow his erratic heart and breathing. The piano he'd heard sat silent in front of him. It and a set of double doors were the only objects on the floor with him. The steel door didn't look very promising with vines spread across the frame in a golden blockade. Even if there was a handle or knob, it wouldn't be as easy as walking inside.

Liam stepped up to the door and drew back a fist, slamming it into the barricade. The metal didn't give way at all. He gnashed his teeth and made a fist once again, this time slamming it into the door even harder. Nothing. The only thing damaged were his bloodied knuckles. His normal methods weren't going to work. How would he get inside? Was there some kind of puzzle he had to solve?

He leaned forward, getting a closer look. The vines rippled and the leaves pulsated as though they were breathing. He ran his fingers along the vine. Thorns suddenly shot out, pricking his fingers. He jerked his hand away.

Liam! Nina's voice called out in thought. But it sounded different. Hollow.

He closed his eyes, reaching for her, trying to pin point where she was within the building. He couldn't find her. Everything was so scrambled. This place didn't have a blueprint that made any sense. Plus, it constantly changed.

He opened his eyes and furrowed his brows at the door. "Let me in!" he bellowed.

The vines glistened and uncoiled, pulling away from the door. Liam stepped back and his eyes widened. The ivy slithered away, pressing against the walls, ceiling, and floor. It couldn't have been that easy.

Liam took a step toward the door, keeping a watchful eye on the ivy. It remained motionless. He took another step forward until he was inches from the doorway. He lifted his foot and without warning the ivy struck.

Vines wrapped around his neck, squeezing as though they were part snake. Liam gasped for air as he clawed at the metal that was literally squeezing the life out of him. Using all his strength, he pulled at the ivy, breaking it off in bits. But right as he pulled one vine off, another took its place. The longer he fought them off, the harder it became to breathe. He didn't know how much more he'd be able to take. Spots appeared before his eyes, and his strength began to wane. He wasn't going to make it. He'd failed. He'd failed his Nina.

His eyes began to close. *I'm so sorry, Nina,* he thought miserably.

Liam!

Liam's eyes sprang open. No. He wasn't done.

"No!" With a strangled scream, he ripped pieces of vine from his neck. They fell around him in lifeless piles. He didn't stop until the floor was littered with golden shreds. Breathless, he fell to his knees, staring at the damage surrounding him.

The door in front of him suddenly popped open, exposing light from within the room it concealed. On wobbly legs, he came to his feet. With a cautious heart, he stepped forward and pushed open the doors.

CHAPTER FORTY

JEREMY SPUN ME AROUND TO CLASSICAL music as he laughed joyfully. I couldn't help but laugh with him. We stopped our waltz, and I smiled up at him. Jeremy caressed my cheek gently with a gloved hand. The adoration behind his eyes was so apparent. How had I not seen it before?

Internally, I shook my head. I struggled to battle against Jeremy's deceptive thoughts that wound through my brain. Somewhere inside I knew it was wrong to be drawn in—a voice inside—was it God's voice—whispered to stand firm, to not give in. Then Jeremy's wheedling, persuasive tones would push it aside. I fought, minute after minute, for what seemed like hours—no—a lifetime, but I felt my control slipping. No matter how hard I fought, I couldn't seem to win. My personality, my will, my thoughts, were becoming enmeshed with Jeremy's, and I was clueless how to stop it from happening.

LIAM IGNORED THE SNAKES striking at the glass beneath his feet and the cloud beasts taunting him overhead. He kept his eyes trained on the purple hallway that stretched out before him. He didn't dare look into the eyes of the people in the painted portraits or into the mirrors. Who knew what fate would befall him if did such a thing. Instead, he ran. He ran as fast as he could.

However, the farther he went, the narrower the hallway became. He stopped for a moment. Hadn't he already seen that picture? And that mirror? He shook his head. No. This place was playing tricks on him. He continued forward. But the hallway seemed to go on and on. He stopped once again, directly in front of the picture he'd seen moments ago. He was going in circles.

He ripped the picture off the wall. A resounding gasp echoed through the hall. Each person within the portraits now held their mouths agape. Liam stabbed his fingers through his hair and leaned against the wall where the picture had hung.

"Liam," a soft voice whispered.

Nina.

He lifted his head and looked into an oval-shaped mirror. Nina stood on the other side of it, staring at him. Excitement shot through his veins, and he stepped forward. His brows furrowed. No, this was another trick.

She cocked her head to the side, giving him a soft smile. Goodness she was beautiful. Even if it wasn't really her. She turned, reaching her hand out to somebody out of his vision. Who was it?

A masculine hand grabbed hold of hers.

Liam's teeth gritted. Jeremy?

The man stepped forward, and Liam's heart leapt into his throat. It wasn't Jeremy. It was Liam. He pulled Nina into his arms. She giggled and leaned back, staring into his eyes.

What was this?

Nina turned her head, looking through the mirror at him. "This could be you. This could be us."

"How?" he whispered.

She nudged her head to her left.

Liam shifted his eyes to the triangle mirror beside hers. His reflection didn't exist. Only blank space stared back at him.

"There's nothing there," he said.

"Look closer."

He stepped up to the mirror and squinted. Ever so slowly, a blue mist started to appear. It grew to the height of the mirror, dancing and swaying as though provoking him.

"All you have to do is allow the Rogues to have access to your soul," Nina said. "To come and go from your earthly body as they choose."

No, he couldn't. He shifted his stare back to Nina and himself within the mirror. They remained in a tight embrace, gazing into each other's eyes. He wanted that. And he could have it.

He looked back to the Rogue. All he had to do was say yes. He swallowed hard and stretched his hand out toward the mirror. A blue tendril reached for him from the other side. Only a couple more inches and he'd be human. Then he'd be free to be with Nina for the rest of their earthly lives.

Liam! Nina's true voice yelled within his thoughts.

He blinked and ripped his hand away from the mirror. What was he doing? "You can't have me," he said to the mist.

The mist growled silently and disappeared.

"Liam!" The fake Nina said within the mirror.

He moved in front of her. The mirror version of himself was gone, and Nina now stood directly in front of him on the other side. Her eyes weren't their normal green, instead they were a cloudy grey full of sadness. And her smile wasn't genuine, it held deceit.

"You aren't my Nina."

Her eyes grew wide with rage. Her lips pulled back revealing teeth as sharp as razors. "You'll never get her back," she said in a deep, rumbling voice that chilled his heart.

"Yes, I will!" He drew his fist back and drove it into the mirror.

Glass rained down around him, and Nina disappeared within the shards that tinkled across the floor. Instead of finding a wall behind the frame of the mirror, there was a dark room. He stuck his head through, but it was pitch black. Should he go in? The purple hallway only continued. And how many more illusions and tricks lay in wait behind the other mirrors? He only had one choice.

Tentatively, he put a foot in, finding a solid floor. So far so good. He stuck his whole body through, but he wasn't standing for long. The floor gave way beneath him. With a scream, he plummeted down. He reached out his hands, searching for a hold, but his fall continued.

Suddenly, he plunged into scalding water. His skin felt as though it were melting. Every stroke to reach the surface was agony. When he finally cut through the surface, he sucked in air wildly. He stared at a single bulb hanging overhead as he swam for the edge. Pulling himself out of the pool took every bit of his strength.

Liam lay on his stomach, breathing deeply and allowing the cool cement to ease his burning skin. His flesh was red and covered in tiny blisters. He gritted his teeth as the blisters faded and his skin returned to its normal bronze.

As soon as he had regained an ounce of strength, he stood and glanced around the cement room. Nothing but the steaming pool was in the room with him. There didn't appear to be doors. He'd had enough. He wasn't even going to bother looking for a way out. He'd make one of his own.

He stepped up to the cement wall and slammed his fist repeatedly. The pain hardly registered as chunks of cement flew every which way, hitting him in his chest, his stomach, his head. He didn't stop until he'd created a hole big enough for him to slide through.

He didn't take the time to glance around the hall into which he'd stepped. Setting his shoulders, he sprinted to an arched door. This one at least had a handle.

With a deep breath, he grabbed hold and pulled. The door opened with ease. He peered in through a small crack. His heart dropped. Nina sat stiff upon a throne in soaking wet sweats and a T-shirt. Keeping his senses open, he walked through into a glorious throne room. He shifted his gaze from side to side. No sign of Jeremy.

Nina looked to Liam, but didn't move. She simply stared at him as though he were a stranger. He approached the throne platform cautiously. Her brows didn't wrinkle, her mouth didn't twitch. Was this even his Nina? Or another trick?

"Nina?"

"Yes, Liam?" she said flatly.

His brows wrinkled. "What are you doing?"

"Waiting for my love to return."

Liam stepped onto the first stair of the platform. "And who might that be?"

"Jeremy, of course."

His stomach churned. Oh, no. He was too late.

Liam knelt in front of her. "Nina, we need to get out of here."

"No. I belong here."

He reached for her hand. She pulled it away. The action made his heart ache. "Nina, this isn't you. Jeremy has used his power of persuasion to convince you to stay."

She shook her head. "I am his queen. He loves me."

"He doesn't. No matter what he said he could give you, this isn't love." He grabbed her arm, pulling her from the throne. "We need to leave. Now."

Nina ripped at his hand. "No! I want to stay!"

"You heard the girl," Jeremy's voice boomed.

Liam jerked his head to the left. Jeremy stepped out from behind a column. Liam hadn't heard him approach. Or perhaps he'd been in the room the whole time, and he hadn't sensed him.

The man truly had become anything but human. With skin as pale as snow and icy eyes that held utter malice and contempt, he exuded an evil Liam had never experienced before.

The corner of Jeremy's mouth curled into an arrogant smile. "Did you enjoy my house of tricks? I was hoping you wouldn't make it through."

Liam's hands fisted. "Nothing will stop me from getting to

Nina."

"I see that now." Jeremy sighed. "Looks like I'll have to kill you myself then." He stopped below the platform.

Liam's heart drummed. "Nina, get behind me."

"She won't listen to you. She's chosen to stay with me."

"It wasn't her choice if you put the thought in her head and convinced her it was her idea."

Jeremy shrugged. "Technicalities." He looked to Nina. "Come here, my dear."

Nina started to walk down the stairs, but Liam clutched her shoulders, turning her to face him. "Nina, listen to me. You don't want to stay."

"Yes, I do." She looked at Jeremy and smiled.

With the palms of his hands firmly pressed against her soft cheeks, Liam turned her head. "You don't. He hurt you. He tried to kill you. Do you remember that?"

"He won't do it again. He loves me."

Jeremy laughed. "You see, Liam. There's nothing you can do to change her mind."

Nina tried to force her head away, but Liam held onto her. His eyes widened as he tried to get her to really hear him. "He doesn't love you. You know who does? Grams and Papa. Lulu. Hezzie. If you stay here, you'll never see any of them again. Is that what you want?"

Her brows wrinkled slightly. "I . . . I don't know."

Jeremy took another step up the platform. "Nina, don't listen to him. Think of all that you'll have here."

Tears filled Nina's eyes.

"You don't love him. He doesn't love you," Liam whispered. "But I do." He pressed his lips to hers, putting all the love and affection he had for her into what could possibly be their last kiss.

A SMALL VOICE WHISPERED within my mind to fight, to wake up, to trust in God. I couldn't do this on my own, and that's what I'd been trying to do all along. It was no wonder I'd been so easily deceived. No one could stand against evil on their own.

With this realization and Liam's lips on mine, everything came into focus. I didn't love Jeremy. I loved the man who was kissing me with such passion that I thought I might melt. I wrapped my arms around Liam's neck, kissing him back.

His lips were suddenly ripped from mine. My eyes opened to find Liam on the floor and Jeremy standing over him. Liam seemed frozen in place. The veins in his neck bulged as he tried to get up.

Jeremy smiled wickedly as his hands fisted. Déjà vu struck as I imagined lightning flashing overhead and Jeremy beating Liam to a bloody pulp. I wouldn't allow that to happen again.

My teeth gritted. Jeremy had somehow convinced me—or tricked me into believing—that I wanted him. That I wanted to give up everything to be with him. Never again. He had no control over me.

God give me strength!

With a scream, I flung myself onto Jeremy's back. I clawed at his face and his neck as I desperately tried tearing him away from Liam.

Jeremy snarled and ripped me off his back, throwing me across the room as though I were a rag doll. Pain rocketed through my skull as it slammed into a column. I closed my eyes and clutched at my head.

When I opened my eyes, the room spun. Liam was kneeling in front of me, his eyes frantic. "Talk to me. Are you okay?"

"Mmm," I mumbled.

"I'm going to take care of this. Once and for all." He stood, heading toward Jeremy.

What was he going to do? There wasn't a way to beat Jeremy.

He was too strong now. I tried to sit up, but fell back with a dizzy spell. "Liam. Stop."

He either didn't hear me or wasn't listening, because he continued with his fists clenching and unclenching by his sides.

"Here we are again," Jeremy said. "I'm a little less breakable this time." He beckoned Liam with his hands. "Come try and break me."

I managed to sit up, but when I attempted to stand, wooziness caused me to fall against the column.

Liam stopped a few feet in front of Jeremy. "I'm not going to fight you."

"What are you going to do?" He smiled. "Talk me to death?"

"I'm going to heal your evil heart."

Jeremy dropped his head back and cackled. "You're going to what?"

Liam shot his hand out to Jeremy, placing his palm on his chest. Jeremy's smile dropped. He grabbed Liam's wrist and tried to pull it away, but it wouldn't budge.

Liam closed his eyes.

What was he doing?

Jeremy's teeth gritted. "Stop!"

Liam's brows pulled together as though he were in pain. His hand shook and the veins within his arm blackened.

"Liam, stop!" I screamed.

What was happening? If he healed Jeremy's heart, what would happen to Liam?

Jeremy's eyes grew heavy, and somehow his skin even more pale. He swayed as though he were going to pass out. Sweat rolled down Liam's cheeks, the veins in his neck pulsated and turned black.

I scrambled to my feet and ran for Liam. A bright blue light suddenly burst from where the two men stood. I skidded to a stop and threw my arms up to shield my eyes. I peeked through my forearms to find a blue mist swirling around where Jeremy had been. It quickly dissipated.

My heart sank. Liam lay lifeless on the floor.

Not again!

"Liam!" I dropped to my knees beside him. His eyes remained closed. I grabbed hold of his face. "Liam, please talk to me." His veins slowly faded from black to their normal blue hue, but he wasn't coming to.

Tears streamed down my cheeks. This couldn't be happening. Not again. Liam deserved to live, even if he couldn't be part of my life.

The ground suddenly quaked beneath us. I glanced around, watching the columns sway and knock over. The arches cracked and began to crumble.

I wiped my eyes. "Liam, this place is collapsing! Move!" I grabbed him beneath his arms and pulled, but he didn't budge. I shook his shoulders. "Liam!"

"Nina, get out of there," Papa's hollow voice called over the rumbling.

I glanced around. "Papa?"

"The place is coming down. Get out now! Through one of the windows!"

I shook my head. "I can't. I can't leave Liam."

"He'll be fine. Get out!"

I leaned down, planting a kiss on his lips. "Come back to me." I had to believe that I'd find him within the clearing. Just like last time. With everything within me, I ran for one of the stained-glass windows that had already shattered.

I stood on the sill, staring down into a black hole. Where would I land? "I can't do it!"

"Yes, you can, sweet pea," Papa's voice called from somewhere unknown. "Jump. You'll be fine."

I gave one last look at Liam. *Please come back to me.*

I closed my eyes and jumped.

CHAPTER FORTY-ONE

My feet hit the snow-covered ground, and I somersaulted. A loud crash sounded behind me. I spun around, finding the shack caving in on itself.

"Liam!" I crawled toward it, but somebody grabbed my shoulders, holding me back. "Liam's in there!" Tears rolled down my cheeks.

"He'll be okay, Nina," Kimmie said from behind me, pulling me away from the wreckage and into her embrace. "Is Jeremy gone?"

I nodded against her. "I think so. Liam . . . he . . ." I broke off with a sob.

Another hand rested on my shoulder. I leaned away from Kimmie to find Papa looking at me with unshed tears.

My face crumpled and I reached for him, burying my face in his neck. He wrapped his arms around my back. "It's okay. You're okay," he whispered.

"How did you find us?"

"I followed Liam and the others. He told me to stay home, but how could he expect me to do that while my Nina was trapped somewhere?"

I smiled weakly. "So stubborn."

He chuckled. "The apple didn't fall far from the tree."

"Nina," Kimmie said. "We have to destroy the passage."

I leaned away from Papa, catching my breath and wiping at my cheeks. "How?"

Damian stepped forward. "By setting it on fire."

My heart sank. No. They couldn't. "But Liam's still in there."

Damian shook his head. "He's gone back home by now."

I stared at the pile of rubble. What if he hadn't? He could still be lying in there helpless. But the passage needed to be destroyed. If it wasn't, then Rogues would continue to pass through. I had to trust that Liam was okay. Even if he wasn't here with me.

It was then that I noticed the group of people tethered to a tree with a large vine. An intense smell of vinegar caused me to cover my nose. These were the people from the portraits. I recognized many of their faces from the paintings.

My eyes landed on the little boy with black hair. I stood slowly, and inched my way toward him. He glared, staring me down.

"Nina, we really need to destroy the passage. Now," Damian said.

I ignored him. I had to give this a shot. These people were worth saving.

I knelt before the little boy. "Do you recognize me?" He shook his head so lightly I almost didn't catch it.

"You tried to warn me of the bad man. Multiple times."

His scowl softened.

I leaned closer. "He's gone. He can't have power over you anymore."

The boy's brows wrinkled.

I reached my hand out, cupping his pale cheek. "You can choose good. It isn't too late."

Tears filled his eyes. "I choose good," he whispered.

His eyes suddenly widened, and he went very still. A blue haze rose from his body and swirled overhead momentarily before dashing into the rubble.

My mouth dropped open. It was possible. I knew it.

The boy relaxed as though he could finally breathe again. He smiled through his tears.

I looked to the others. "You can choose as well."

They glanced at me and then looked to each other, trying to decide what to do.

"I choose good," an older gentleman said.

"I choose good," a young woman chimed.

One by one, they each proclaimed their choice. Angry blue fog filled the air, whizzing every which way until it found the passage.

They were free.

"Now," Damian declared.

Violet stood beside the debris with a torch in hand. Kimmie and Damian stepped up beside her. Violet leaned down, setting the wood on fire. The three Martyrs joined hands and closed their eyes. Together they repeated, "The evil man has no future, the lamp of the wicked will be put out."

The flames grew taller as they consumed the remains. It wasn't long before the shack and everything within it was reduced to ash.

CHAPTER FORTY-TWO

GRAMS HELD A HANKIE TO HER mouth, and she cried tears of joy from the back porch as she watched Papa and me come up to the house. As soon as we reached the porch, she pulled me into a tight embrace. "Oh my sweet Nina. Is it over?"

I nodded. "It's over."

"Thank the Lord." She leaned back, smiling as she lightly stroked my cheek. She looked to Papa, her smile turning to a scowl. "I told your grandpa not to go after you, but of course he didn't listen."

He shot her a look of innocence. "I helped get her back, didn't I?"

Grams eyes widened, and she turned to me. "Where's Liam?"

My mouth dropped into a frown. "I'm not sure where he is at the moment."

Her brows pulled together. "What do you mean?"

I bit down on my lip briefly then released it. "It's complicated. But I'll see him soon." At least I hoped I would. I glanced at the setting sun. I hadn't realized how late it was. I needed to hurry if I was going to make it to the clearing on time.

I hopped down from the porch. "I'll see you guys in a couple of hours."

"Where are you going?" Papa asked.

Walking backwards, I looked to my grandparents. "To the pond."

"Is that a good idea? Is it safe?" Grams asked.

I smiled. "I'm safer now than I've been in years. I'll be back soon." With that, I spun around and sprinted for the barn. When I entered the stable, I threw my arms around Hezzie's neck then saddled him so fast I could have won an award.

Hezzie took off as soon as I swung onto his back, automatically heading in the direction of the clearing. My heart raced with anticipation. Only a matter of minutes and I'd be in Liam's arms again. My stomach suddenly clenched. What if he wasn't there? What if this time was different, and he wouldn't be allowed to visit me again?

I dug my heels in Hezzie's sides, pushing him to go faster. We reached the tree row, and I slid off his back. I realized I still wore my soggy sweats and T-shirt. And my hair was a frizzy mess. But it didn't matter. Liam wouldn't care. Still, I ran my fingers through my hair and tried to straighten myself up a bit.

With butterflies fluttering in my stomach, I pushed through the trees. Liam wasn't present yet. I popped my knuckles. It was okay. He'd be here. The sun hadn't quite set yet. He still had time. But the farther the sun dropped and the darker the sky became, the more my stomach somersaulted.

I paced the dry grass of the clearing, waiting for it to suddenly turn lush and green. The sun completely dropped, and the moon took its place in the dark sky. Something was wrong. What if Kimmie was mistaken? What if Liam didn't make it out of the shack? I continued to wait for him, but my hope waned with every minute he didn't show.

By the end of the two hours, I lost all hope. I sank down onto the ground and pulled my knees to my chest. My throat tightened as I tried to hold back my tears. I couldn't let them free. They'd never stop. I closed my eyes and rocked back and forth.

Oh, God, please comfort me. I can't take the heartbreak.

My eyes popped open at the sound of Hezzie's whinny. I sprang to my feet as rustling sounded in the trees. My heart raced and I prepared myself to run. Even though Jeremy was gone and the passage had been destroyed, paranoia was inevitable.

"Who's there?" I called.

A dark figure stepped through. I screamed and took off in the other direction.

"Nina, wait!" Liam called.

My heart leapt. I stopped and spun around, squinting into the darkness. He came closer until I could see his face.

"Liam!" I squealed as I ran to him. I jumped into his arms and he tumbled backward, falling to the ground. I covered his face with kisses. "Where were you? I was worried sick." I leaned away to get a better look at him. "Wait a minute. Why did you come through the trees? And how was I able to take you down?"

A grin spread across his face.

I glanced around the clearing, realizing the grass was still dead and cold, and no flowers poked through. I returned my attention to Liam. "What's going on?"

Liam grabbed my hands, pulling me with him to stand. "Do you have anything you need healed?"

I eyed him suspiciously. "No. Why?"

"Because I can't."

"Excuse me?"

His smile deepened. "I'm human."

My eyes widened. "What? How?"

"I was rewarded for going beyond my assigned duties. The Martyr High Council praised me for giving myself to the cause. They asked what they could do for me in return. I didn't expect them to grant my request."

I squeezed his hands. "What does this mean then?"

"What do you want it to mean?"

I grinned as I pictured our life. Marriage, a family, growing old together. Joy coursed through my body. "I want a long future with you."

He beamed. "Agreed."

I couldn't bottle up the questions bombarding my mind any

longer. "What happened to you after I left the passage? Where are Kimmie, Damian, and Violet? And what—"

Liam's lips were suddenly on mine, silencing my questions. All my inquisitions melted away.

Liam pulled away. "We can get to your questions soon. We have plenty of time."

That we did. No more two-hour regulation! I could spend every moment with him anywhere I wanted. I cupped Liam's jaws with both hands. "Well." I came to my toes and planted a quick kiss on his lips. "Here's looking at you, kid."

He chuckled. "What's that mean?"

"It's from the movie Casablanca. A classic."

Liam leaned down, planting his lips on mine again. Kisses in romance movies had nothing on the way he kissed. His lips left mine and tingles shot through my body. He caressed my cheek with his knuckles. "We have a lot of movies for me to catch up on."

I smiled. "That we do. Shall we get started?"

With a laugh, I grabbed his hand and tugged him through the trees. Liam helped me onto Hezzie's back, and he hopped on behind me. I leaned into him as he wrapped his arms around my middle. I closed my eyes, savoring the feeling of being in his mortal arms.

Satan had wanted to destroy me all this time. First through Jeremy, then through the deceit of a Rogue. I'd gone through more than my share of spiritual warfare. But God gave me strength and sent Liam to save me, in more ways than one. Liam being willing to die yet again had been love's supreme sacrifice.

Liam kissed my temple. "Now that I'm human, I'll probably need to find a job. Perhaps I'd

make a good farm hand." He squeezed my waist. "We could harvest and take care of the horses together forever. Can you picture it?"

I nodded against his chest. "It sounds perfect."

I truly could see it. Vividly. And it was beautiful.

Author Note

Dear Reader,

Spiritual warfare is very real and very scary. In fact, I experienced it in the midst of writing *Love's Sacrifice*. Satan didn't want the message of this story to get out, so he attacked me. He did so by preying on my depression. He knew that by making me plunge into a pit, I wouldn't want to write. And boy did it work. I went weeks without writing and any time I sat in front of the computer to do so, I felt an overwhelming amount of sadness.

The message that I hope you heard in this story is that the enemy can come in many forms. He can make us believe that only he can fulfill the desires of our hearts. However, he puts a veil over our eyes and masks the true evil within those longings. The Bible says that Satan disguises himself as an angel of light. Satan has and always will use this disguise to tempt believers and non-believers to stray from God. It can be something as simple as a sinful thought, to something as major as a horrific crime.

Ephesians 6:11 says, "Put on the full armor of God, so that you will be able to stand firm against the schemes of the devil." But how do we do that? Of course, going to church and surrounding yourself with believers can help guard you from the enemy. But ultimately prayer is what helped me. Calling out to God pulled me out of Satan's grasp.

My prayer for all my readers is that if you don't know God personally, then you will seek him out. I guarantee he's been waiting for you. If you do know God, I pray that you always reach out to and rely on him.

God loves you. Always has and always will. No matter what. Never forget that.

Sincerely,
Kelsey Norman

Made in the USA
Monee, IL
14 February 2022